CW00496021

MR COLES

Also by Simon Astaire

Private Privilege

And You Are …?

MR COLES

Simon Astaire

For Leo co Jess
my dearest friends
with love

QUARTET

Simon

January 26th
2014

First published in 2011 by
Quartet Books Limited
A member of the Namara Group
27 Goodge Street, London W1T 2LD

A catalogue record for this book
is available from the British Library

ISBN   978 0 7043 7215 3

Typeset in Great Britain by Antony Gray
Printed and bound by T J International Ltd,
Padstow, Cornwall

To those who have suffered
but were unable to tell anyone.

ACKNOWLEDGEMENTS

For M. J. M. for the use and guidance of his journals. To D. A. for her belief and for her love. To J. C. for his advice and patience. For G. M. S. for encouragement and friendship. To C. B. for the Valentine's dinner. To M. V. for her unwavering support. To A. B. for remembrance of things past. To P. L. for that save. For S. B. for his humour. And of course to my son Milo, thank you.

PROLOGUE

It was, it is me. I take responsibility for all that has happened. I love my arrogance that anyone should be remotely interested to read my revelations. Who should care! I recall the events in the cool sobriety of dawn. But it is as if I have been a funfair sideshow where I have somehow tossed a ring over my individuality. I had, as it were, stirred a shoal of brain cells in my mind that had lain dormant for years. I have tried to capture, to pinpoint such moments that resonate even today. Some that had gone missing presumed drowned. There will be times when I wish to speak to you directly and perhaps with a shhh, perhaps confidentially. I am not sure how best to do this other than just do it with no interruptions and with a pace that the modern mind needs and requires – action, action, action. Many people find any interruption aggravating – especially I have noticed those who do not know how to use the word properly. What do they say; once a teacher always a teacher! Yet one of the purposes of leaving these thoughts open to be scrutinised is that I need to make peace with myself or free myself from the bondage of thought. I will at times congratulate myself on being correct in my action and having the right to defend my own definition of each and every thing.

PART ONE

THE SILENCE of the empty school always drove me insane. I opened my eyes and was immediately wide awake – a long night soaked in oblivion. I felt numbness somewhere above my neck, my mind pickled, throat dry as a desert. I needed company – I admit that. I needed the sound of the boys, sleeping soundly and sweetly just a heartbeat from my door. I never could enjoy the secure sleep of a child, even when I was a child. I learned young, when I felt most tired, I slept least well. I thought it strange when I was wide awake, I would be sent to bed and expected to go straight to sleep, without question and turn myself off with the light. How cruel! And then, at some unearthly hour of the morning, I was awoken from my dreams and expected to be alert in an instant, without murmur. 'Shoosh,' I was told if I complained. Just another piece to the jigsaw called 'I am who I am'.

The headmaster, an ex-army man, called me into his office after the morning staff meeting. 'Mr Coles, please join me, if you have time?' he said, heels clicking together, no doubt to give some of his full-blooded headmasterly advice. He always plugged his platitudes with a quotation or misquotation: 'Make yourself honey and flies will eat you,' or, 'He was so generally civil that no one thanked him.'

His desk was in front of large bay windows, red plush

curtains hanging down at each end. There was a disused bell-pull by a marble fireplace that made the heat of the room intolerable when lit. The headmaster sat at his desk amidst scattered reports and an old fashioned black telephone; the kind which weighs a ton and gives the impression there won't be any quick calls.

He was about to speak but then let himself be distracted as if he had much more important matters to attend to. He unscrewed the top of his Parker pen, signed some papers in his gothic hand like tracks of a prize skater on a melting ice rink, blotted, and handed them to his scurrying shrew-like secretary. 'Letter to the governors,' he said in a confidential tone. 'Would you mind helping me welcome the new boys this evening, Coles? I can't think of anyone more charming to have by my side.'

'Of course, headmaster.' I didn't want to exaggerate my good mood or he would guess how shit I felt, much like most of the time. He then talked up timetables and, whilst doing so, buttoned up his woollen cardigan although it was still very warm outside. He noticed my surprise. 'I feel the cold, goes back to being a child. One night I was left to fend for myself on a lonely moor in the middle of winter, but that is another story . . . ' he said.

Yes, let's not go into that one again, headmaster.

The gist of our conversation was that I would be taking History and French with 2A, the Common Entrance year, and with 3B and 3C. The headmaster would teach Form One (the scholars) French. I would be in charge of the Colts for football and next term, the Colts for rugger. It was what I expected – nothing more, nothing less – rather like life.

'Merci, Monsieur Coles. À tout à l'heure,' he said, rather too loudly for someone standing inches away.

'Yes thank you very much, headmaster, sir.' I never forgot the 'sir'. I stood up and shook his hand, leaving with a niggling feeling that he would do well to retire soon before suffering something of a coronary. His face was very grey, his handshake damp and limp.

As I walked through the corridor towards the staff room, the new geography master breezed up to make a formal introduction. He was a strange type. I had a suspicion that there was an antipathy between art and life. It was just instinct but I thought he held a secret. We spoke as we walked around the freshly cut First XI pitch, smoking my cigarettes. Our conversation was intermediately broken by his deep sighs. He had started to write a novel about his school days and was finding it very painful: bold admission for a first meeting. We promised to meet for a drink at the weekend. Perhaps he recognised something that stirred a longing to be open? Fear is what keeps secrets secret.

The staff room had been rubbed with polish. The school photos straightened and piles of letters had been sorted with practised efficiency into three groups: the staff, headmaster, and the boys. The third pile was the largest. Parents sent letters to welcome their sons for the new term as well those left behind from the end of the summer. The art teacher had the most correspondence – young, handsome, foolish and in demand. I don't give him long here. He seemed far too 'nice' to have the stamina to see life through as a prep school master. I understood he had a lover in London. We had not seen her yet but I had heard him on the phone, purring with his self-satisfied middle morality lips: 'Darling one, I miss you so.' Sounds as if I am jealous – of course I am, but I won't waste too much energy on that.

I was sitting in my wicker chair admiring the picture I had bought near to Bournemouth Station a few weeks before. Packed trains screaming a working class snort as they pulled up to drop the English for their summer holidays. Even above the noise of the train itself I could hear the babble of over-excited people streaming on, in wave after wave of indiscriminate nonsense. 'They sound the horn, to make everyone feel like they're on bloody holiday,' the owner of the hidden gallery grumbled. I immediately recognised a kindred spirit; another moaner.

On the wall was a drawing of an androgynous creature wrapped in a white sheet; a wolf in snow. I was startled at its splendour and stood motionless. There is no need to rush anything in life – the essence of a sound mind is to remain still. Yes I wanted it; I wanted it on my wall; not above the bed but to the left of my desk. Yes, that would be fine. The moaner gave a good price, no haggling needed. 'It will make you very happy,' he snorted. I gave him a slight frown within my smile and walked out. I did not know what the scoundrel meant.

Falling asleep mid afternoon is never a good idea. I looked at my watch, 'Shit!' It was five o'clock and the parents would be arriving within the hour. This was no time to slack; I leapt up like a man late for his own wedding.

I went to my washbasin and set about shaving. Best to shave again, wanted to look my best for headmaster and parents and in that order. I hummed 'Onward Christian Soldiers' and looked closely at my eyes in the mirror. Clear as a cloudless summer day. What a relief, the lunchtime gin had no effect on mind or body. I cut precariously through thick lather with a sharp razor; I liked the sense of danger, the possibility of a cut. But there wasn't to be one, not a single cut, no blood. I admired my clean shave. As a way of celebration, I swigged a tot of alcohol from my flask, or was it two shots? Then brushed my teeth – no tell-tale gin breath on me.

My ironed white shirt fell from the sad-looking wire hanger. I promised that day I was going to make my presence felt. The headmaster would see how well I socialised, a true asset to the school. Yes, I am ambitious and indeed rejuvenated, reborn – made young again. Mind you, the strong aftershave helped. It stung horribly and I shook my face from right to left and from left to right enjoying the pain without sound.

I chose my very best suit, my only suit – navy blue, ministerial and with matching socks. The brown brogues may have let the side down but that could be seen as a sign of eccentricity. Yes that is what I am, an eccentric. My old college tie, as usual, gave the air of authority – very important. I combed my hair with my metallic toothcomb – it is always matted and painful to tidy. I must remember to buy that brush which has been gathering dust in the local chemist's front window. Perhaps the miserable Mr Patel will knock off a quid from its exorbitant price? Though I doubted it, the mean sod!

I had given myself one more look in the mirror and was about to head downstairs when I heard an efficient sounding knock on my door. I felt a surge of panic like a schoolboy examinee that has left his revision all too late.

'Mr Coles are you ready?' It was the head just passing by.

'I am ready, sir,' I sidled out of my room and locked the door behind as he peered over his shoulder.

The parents had not yet arrived by the time we had reached the library. The sandwiches neatly lined on three rather grand plates, teapots still empty and a rather dreary collection of biscuits. A bottle of whiskey stood alone with two glasses either side.

'The occasional parent sometimes asks for something stronger than a cup of tea. Best to be prepared,' the headmaster advised, catching my gaze, 'very rare though.' My plastic smile returned and I walked away from any sudden temptation. 'You wait here and I'll stand by the front door,' he ordered.

Twenty new boys arrived, an encouraging intake for the governors; there was a fear that numbers were dwindling. The sons of the prosperous upper-middle class trooped in one by one and I put my arm forward to greet and welcome them.

'Hello and welcome to Falston.' It was as if I had been doing this for years.

'My you're an attractive fellow,' remarked a mother moving towards me across the room, slow as an evening shadow; black blood choking the varicose veins that crossed her mountainous legs.

'Thank you,' I answered modestly, shrugging my shoulders with the nonchalance of a man who had heard it all before.

'Ah, what a handsome chap,' our neighbours had cooed.

My mother would never answer directly, instead she simply replied, 'He was all I ever wanted' and then whisper into my ear, 'my beautiful son.' My father, whose mood depended on the number of invitations on his mantle piece, received any compliment bestowed on his boy as a personal tribute. 'He looks just as I did when I was his age.'

'Come here and meet your handsome teacher,' the pushy mother chided; but the boy was having none of it. Feeling shy and insecure, he pushed her away and seemed to sulk.

There was silence followed by the boy running back to the protection of his mother's side.

'He is a good chap really.'

Of course he is.

'I promise he will be happy here at Falston. I will personally keep my eye on him.' She smiled conspiratorially at my reassurance and whispered a 'thank you'. I walked away surveying the room. What a remarkably dreary bunch. But there is always an exception.

Quite suddenly, I noticed a navy blue Bentley pulling up to the front. I was immediately alerted to something different – wealth and style removed from the dull collection of Volvos. A flicker of suspicion crossed the eyes of those in the room. The new arrivals were the sort one sees in the street and immediately thinks too much money. Not me mind you. My first thought is how do they spend it, and close second, why don't they give more of it away? To me, for instance. I left the mediocrity to have a closer look; the mother was slim, long-legged and with a hard, clear-cut ethereal beauty that one sees in beauty advertisements. The father handsome, tailored with strong shoulders, and their son, walking nervously behind, was as freshly beautiful as April with a glossy mane of lustrous brown hair; he had rose and ivory cheeks.

It took time for them to make an entrance, the headmaster was clearly buttering them up; he was good at working the room.

'May I introduce myself?' were my first words. The mother offered her hand, her fragrance only emphasising her beauty.

'How do you do? I am Constance and this is my son.'

D was unsure whether to offer his hand. All new boys present a sense of isolation but D was different. He drew a deep breath and shook my hand with strength. I could see immediately that he needed comfort. I told him that I was the history teacher but he was still too young to be taught by me. I was about to ask whether he liked cricket when his father interrupted into our conversation and dragged him away to look at a shitty portrait of one of the late headmasters. I felt disheartened as the feeling of being unwanted turned my mood and a wave of tiredness swept over me. As D walked away with his father, I had an urge to snap at his parents for the intrusion: 'How dare you barge in like that?' But the feeling soon subsided, as I knew they would be returning to London and their son would remain in my care. I should have left it there; allow D to have a quiet moment with his father but something – I am not sure what – propelled me to join their conversation. Perhaps I was just being pushy or not pushy enough? I was about to impress them with my knowledge of the history of Falston, 1907 to present day, when the head began his customary 'It's the finest Prep School in England' speech – tiresome after the fiftieth time of hearing, but impressive at the first. I caught D's eye as the head was waffling on and mouthed the word that says everything, 'OK?' He smiled shyly back and I felt a longing to stand by his side.

It ended with the headmaster announcing, 'You have ten minutes to say your goodbyes.' The parents then walked to their cars, back into the fresh air, adjusting their eyes and minds to the outside world.

'Come on. It isn't that bad. Be like your father, be brave,' I said to D cheerily, to which the headmaster gave me a sharp look. Oh dear!

'Look after him, won't you?' D's mother, or was it his father, asked.

'Of course,' I replied in my practised Mr Niceness tone. 'I promise he will be happy here at Falston. I'll personally keep my eye on him.'

I desperately wanted to withdraw back to my room to swig some sherry, hidden for just such an emergency under the socks in the top drawer, but I didn't think I had time. I was on dinner duty, and as the new boys were saying their goodbyes, the rest of the school seemed to arrive all at once.

The bell rang as tradition required, its continual sound was meant to send a huge welcome to everyone. When I'm head, it will be the first tradition to be binned.

The corridors and stairs were soon bursting, young faces pushing past asking whether I'd had a good holiday. No I fucking didn't. The bell relented and was swiftly overtaken by the boys exuberant squealing at the top of their voices, pushing and pinching as the crowd jostled this way and that. I tried vainly to introduce some order into the rabble. 'Not so fast boy,' or 'get a bloody move on you lazy git.' The last days of their pampered summer had come abruptly to a close; no self pity allowed here.

I did manage to get that swig of that sherry before dinner, in fact, two full glasses and in the process I missed evening prayers. I returned to the dining room just in time for the headmaster's recital, for the second outing of the Lord's Prayer, accompanied by the droning tones of a hundred boys. The Irish stew was devoured immediately by the boys with their bottomless healthy appetites; so much for the complaints of school dinners.

Jackson was the new head boy and he approached with a stern expression. 'I hope you will call upon me if you need any help, sir,' he said, as if addressing the captain of his platoon. You know exactly how his life will turn out: Army followed by marriage, two kids and death in front of the television – a sturdy little chap though, middle-aged by his thirteenth birthday.

'Thank you, Jackson,' I said.

Early to bed, the boys trooped up the stairs and down the corridors, to the long dormitories. The juniors were on the first floor and the more senior on the second. The bathroom was packed with juniors eagerly scrubbing off the dirt with a bowl of cold water and drying with a clean towel. They had a blend of looks on their pretty faces, some confident, others with sorrow. I caught one staring out of the window, counting clouds, oblivious to where he was and seemingly astonished when I whispered into his ear that he'd better get a move on.

The more senior boys were casual in their approach, discussing their holidays and spending minute upon minute brushing their teeth and grooming themselves. I left the head boy and senior monitor in charge and made my way to 'Middle Dorm' to find D, to wish him well for his first night as a boarder. I may be a callous bastard but even I can be empathetic to the first night away from home. I had been sent to my prep school when I was eight so the memory was not so distant. As I walked, I felt an attack of cramp run up – or is it down – my leg. My left leg was cocked at a right angle. I was always led to believe that cramp was the first sign of decline. I paused at the junction of corridors and craned my neck round the corner to make sure no one was watching. One of the senior boys was heading in my direction, so I took a coin out of my pocket and threw it to the ground.

'Pick that up boy?'

'Of course, sir . . . is everything OK, sir?'

'Why shouldn't it be?'

I sighed to the world and told him to get a 'bloody move on'.

I eventually found his small figure with those unmistakable brown locks of hair lying face up; staring at the ceiling with a small bear draped on his shoulder.

'It does get better you know, be strong now,' I said and sentimentally reached down to stroke away the frown from his brow. I think he murmured a 'thank you' and then turned his back.

During the summer months I had forgotten how tiring a tribe of boys can be. When I returned to my room, I poured myself a drink, lifted my feet up onto my desk, and looked at my drawing. Although the school was still, I imagined the sound of insistent knocking; it grew like a pulse on the brain. Everything seemed a little too much. I poured my last shot of whiskey to help relieve my solitude. 'I don't want to sleep alone for the rest of my life,' were the last thoughts of the day.

1973

I caught young what's-his-name with bloodshot eyes: 'Tears?' I asked, as he pressed his blackheads against the bathroom mirror. The poor fellow was just thirteen and covered in spots. He would be off to Eton in no time. It is hard enough to fit in to a school like that; harder still if you're not pretty. It seems the beautiful get as much as they want, the less beautiful don't. I have also discovered in life that the very beautiful stay alone and are therefore ripe for picking.

'Don't be vain so young, it is exhausting,' I said. These boys generally remain strong until they're about eighteen and then they begin to fall like skittles to the rigours of the outside world. Some, like this boy in particular, may fall earlier. Do they not realise that school days are the best days of their lives? Not so much as a worry, all taken care of, except if you have acne and then no one can help – not Clearasil, Quinaderm, nothing! Just bloody Mother Nature taking her turn with the glands. I am tempted to add condolences, 'Don't worry lad, they will clear up soon . . . it happens to the best of us.' But I don't, as I never liked the swine.

'Hurry up spotty, first game on First XV pitch, don't keep us all waiting,' I yelled.

'But I am in the second match, sir,' he answered.

'Don't answer back!'

I was in charge of rugby and it was the annual seven-a-side touch rugby competition. Always a chance for major injuries as the young boys joined the old. Spotty had young D on his side and I was the referee. Fawning parents had made the effort to come and support their sons. Good for them! No sign of D's parents though. Good for them!

I placed the ball in the middle of the field, and watched the second hand of my rather ostentatious sports watch tick down. The boys stood stationary like cattle keeping a patch of ground dry in readiness for rain. I emptied my throat with a coarse cough, blew my whistle and suddenly a mad surge of pubescent boys yelled and ran after each other; let it begin. D was a born sportsman and was growing before my very eyes. Long limbed, with long jumps he avoided tackles with ultimate ease. He was truly beautiful to watch, like a cheetah in full flight; life could not have been better.

Half-time and I knew it was simply not right but I whispered a 'well played' to D as the teams swapped halves. Mostyn, the opposing captain overheard and gave out a mock 'boo' or a noise that was a secret code to convey his displeasure. Bugger off, we can all have our favourites! It might have been a figment of my tired imagination but I believed Mostyn sulked for the rest of the game. I very nearly sent him off when he deliberately manhandled young D who was charging down the wing. A wallop and thump went in his tackle. Spoilt little shit! This was meant to be 'touch' rugby for God's sake. I called him over and told him off with my finger in his face and a stern word. Not too harsh though, as his overbearing fat 'not so bright' father was standing on the touchline.

'See me after dinner boy,' I said and he marched away with a smug smile, content that he had caught my attention. His father offered a word of consolation to his son after their crashing defeat. Young D emerged the hero of the game with three tries. Mostyn shoved him off with a 'leave me alone' spoilt push. His father, seeing that I had seen the minor altercation, nodded as if to say 'deal with him later won't you?'

I certainly will, sir.

D's seven was eventually beaten in the final. It turned out to be very one-sided, 54–6, so there was no point in helping to sway the result. The head of the governors presented the trophy with what sounded like a very unsuitable comment:

'To see the fitness in these young men is a wonder to behold.' He tapped his midriff, 'I congratulate you all. The winning team is . . . ' and up marched Master Templeton Stanley, first XV captain, school hero and overall 'good egg' to everyone but me. He accepted the trophy, offered a proud handshake, and lapped up the ovation. I do not like him. He makes my skin crawl with his swagger and salacious innuendos to his juniors. I notice, as I grow older, that I like hardly anybody. Love, maybe. Like, impossible. I have an instinctive loathing for most. I don't confront unless I have to, I move to the other side of the room. Maybe not the best qualification for a schoolmaster but I don't doubt my ability to teach, never that. Two hours of my tuition and a boy will be on his way to learning more than the average British imbecile child.

I took out a cigarette, tapped the end on the palm of my hand, lit and smoked. Did I hear one of the parent's tutting?

'Not in front of the boys!' she chided.

'Charming,' I thought, and blew a plume of smoke in the direction of the spoiler. The type that complains that there should be no smoking at all – full stop! Surely smoking out in the open is doing no harm? But I admit I will punish any boy encouraging anyone else to smoke for the first time. They will be punished in the appropriate manner, a whack of the slipper firmly on the backside. Now does that make you feel better dear parent? Let's just say that some of us need a little something to relieve the drudgery of life and soothe away the daily stress.

The boys bathed and showered before gathering for tea. I went up to the shower room to find the geography master standing guard.

'Hurry up boys!' I heard him order. Hmmm, what was it that made his words seem insincere?

'That is quite enough,' I said. 'I will take over here.' The geography master looked surprised. 'Get your hands out of your pockets,' I demanded.

'But it is my turn to be here,' he replied, lips pursed.

'My turn to be here,' I mimicked, and with disdain. 'You are not a bloody child. Good day to you.' He looked at me as if I were a dead rat held by the tail.

The showers were a den of iniquity or a den of potential iniquity – if there were no master in charge. The fight for towels and who bagged the soap could turn into one big tes-tosterone tussle, a veritable Bacchanalian orgy. The shy would slink into the corner whilst the seducers would take centre stage showing off to the others. I stood motionless as the steam half-protected the boys from those prying eyes, the voyeur in all of us. God, I needed a drink, its absence dis-tracted me from wondering what I was doing there in the first place. Anything, even the roughest plonk would do. After the first taste of alcohol, anything that follows becomes tolerable. Does that define me as an alcoholic? I was having this debate with myself, when D emerged from the shower in search of his towel. Some bully had stolen it. The poor beautiful child shivered.

'Who has this boy's towel?' Righteous anger grew by the second; my irritation igniting into rage. 'I said who has his towel? Can't you see he is cold . . . ?' D was pointing to my left hand, which had remained still as I gesticulated with my right. 'What is it child?' His damp white towel dangled from my clenched fingers. Dear God, I must have picked it up as he walked into the shower; and I, caught out by my own subconscious.

'Oh is this yours?' I asked nonchalantly. I did not betray a hint of irony in my question.

I made a quick exit to the sanctity of my room. I reached beneath my pillow and grabbed for the bottle. Hell, I was thirsty. A long deep slug – that was better; I immediately felt revived. I lit the fire from a replenished bag of logs that I had bought earlier in the week from the bored Mr Luckhurst close to the station. He does not like me. When I politely asked whether I could have one of those old-fashioned coal bags to carry the logs, he looked straight into my eyes and spat, 'No you can't!' Charming! I won't be using him again.

One strike of the match triggered the wood into an explosion of warmth. My behaviour earlier had given concern. I must not lose control. As they say: 'you give yourself away by running too fast.'

I am convinced I am developing an awful squint. Not sure who to ask whether it is true or simply paranoia setting in each time I look in the mirror. I am also angry that my eagerness to watch over the showers distracted me from 'schmoozing' with the head of governors. I am not content to be just another teacher here. Oh no not me! My ambitions are far greater. I will be headmaster of Falston one day.

There was a knock at the door. I kept quiet. It was the geography master. 'Are you there Coles? I say Coles are you there?' I stood motionless. I could smell his aftershave waft under the door. It was the smell of lavender, not unlike the scent my grandmother used to wear; the associations of life. I kept glued to my wall repeating quietly to myself, 'Go away and leave me alone', and indeed he did, much to my relief. Ten minutes later, there was another knock. Again I stood still and heard a faint voice. 'It is Mostyn, sir!'

Mostyn, I thought, remembering the dressing down I had given him earlier that afternoon.

'Oh yes Mostyn, come on in,' I unlocked my door. The boy was in his pyjamas, dressing gown tied tight around him. I looked at my watch as the memories came flooding back of a time I had travelled to visit a friend of my father's who lived just outside Nairobi. Each evening was still, except for a faint murmur of a transistor radio clashing with a symphony of insects that swarmed in the garden. It was odd they only seemed to come out at night.

*   *   *

The headmaster thought it was a bravo idea.

'We don't encourage the younger ones to take the leading roles but I think this time we will make an exception. Anyway, you are the director and I respect your taste and choice.'

'Fine, headmaster, I will tell him.'

Our latest school play was to be the farcical black comedy *Arsenic and Old Lace*. A strange choice indeed, but it was the headmaster and his wife's favourite movie. After a brief debate, it was decided that this would be the play and not my choice of *The Mikado*.

'You decide on this year's play,' the headmaster had said before the holidays, but his words were hollow.

I had cast D to play the part of the hapless Mortimer, nephew to the murderess aunts. I was going to tell him before he retired to bed but I lost my nerve. It is hard to admit that someone so youthful can have this effect. I avoid temptation because once you take a first step you will continue in the same way for life. I suppose I am playing with the proverb, 'Once you have given once, you must give all your life.'

Fighting broke out in the dining room earlier that evening. D had hurled himself at nasally Owen Thomas, for stealing a sausage off his plate. D has a boarding house approach to his food; he craves every last crumb. I have seen the way he eats – like a condemned man at his last supper. I wanted to tell him to take it easy and play father with my advice: 'There will be many more meals to come in your life.' He had given Owen Thomas a bloody nose, blood had poured onto his shirt. I noticed a rare blush of satisfaction painted on D's face. In fantasy, I had wanted the fight to continue to the bitter- sweet end and for D to maim his opponent or even to kill him: 'Can killing ever be justified?' 'Is Death truly sometimes a solution or a need?' Maybe, but I should continue to remember that just because someone dies for something, it does not necessarily mean that that someone and something were right.

I could not let the fight go without discipline and ordered D to leave the rest of his dinner and have a bath before bed.

'Hurry upstairs and finish your prep,' I snapped like a sergeant major. 'And you, Owen Thomas, go up, change and come back to finish your dinner.'

I absent-mindedly forgot to say grace before dinner; so I rang the bell that sits on the top table and asked the school to clasp their hands together – to look forward and say grace.

> Benedic, Domine, nos et dona tua,
> quae de largitate tua sumus sumpturi,
> et concede, ut illis salubriter nutriti
> tibi debitum obsequium praestare valeamus,
> per Christum Dominum nostrum.

One hundred muffled 'Amen's' followed. 'All right then, dismissed.'

When Owen Thomas returned I asked what had caused the stir. 'He called me a "name",' he replied. I knew the wretch was lying but did not question his lame excuse, he had after all been the one covered in blood. 'You can change tables tomorrow, Owen Thomas,' I said.

'Yes please, sir – which one, sir?' There was desperation in his voice.

Sitting next to D can't be that bad? Owen Thomas should

remember that if he changes tables mid-term, or has one chosen for him, he might be sat with someone who eats soup through his nose or does strange things with his hands and legs out of view. 'Be careful young man; give yourself time before making a rash choice of this kind.' I told him that he would find out what table he would be sitting on the following day and made a mental note to banish him to the far reaches of the dining room.

That night, I breathed deeply and sighed. I felt liberated being in charge of the school. The headmaster and the under master, Mr Collett, had to attend some dreadful dinner at Westminster. It's how the system works, public schools court each other for potential A-grade students. The evening will be dull conversation, too much wine, and much social chitchat. It will all be different when I come to represent the school. I will be the life and soul of the party, making effort, effortlessly. 'Yes Mister Coles, brilliant hypothesis Mr Coles, we are so lucky to have you in the club Mr Coles.'

Yes I see it now, first headmaster of Falston, followed by Eton, Harrow, or even Haileybury; I don't mind where, as long as I am appreciated.

My last duty of the night was to make sure the boys, *in puris naturalibus*, were properly bathed. It was usually Matron's job but she had been called away this evening and would be returning late; I was, of course, the most willing volunteer to cover for her.

The bathroom was a medley of noise, water, vanity, and nudity, not in that order. I recoiled as D walked into his bath, making sure that I never repeated my atrocious behaviour with the towel in the showers. And yet for an instant I thought I was audibly musing and meowing like a cat. It had to be our secret; D smiled and made a fuss of the water's temperature like a sly tart. Secretly, I devoured his perfect body. Did anyone see my furtive glances? Of course not, I was far too clever for that. My conscience still stuttered banalities in my head and I found myself on the defensive. What I needed was a drink to stiffen my resolve.

D splashed water over his shoulders, I was unable to move, mesmerised by his adolescent beauty, the desire almost palpable. The water evaporated into D's cream skin, slowly drifting from sight. Oh, to be with him – the craving was vicious enough to kill for. The sound of Matron's shrill tones shook me out of my reverie. She had returned early.

'Hurry them up, Mr Coles. These boys should be in bed now,' Matron, all witchlike and spiky, snapped her fingers in annoyance.

I was caught – a lone spectator. Stuttering as if punch drunk, I demanded that they all got out immediately. Water surged over the deep baths and soaked the stone floor. I could not stand it anymore and turned away to the far door to check on something that did not exist. The smell of toothpaste soothed my state and for an instant I caught sight of my face in one of the mirrors. I stopped dead in my tracks, eyes resolutely in front. My face had aged; hair damp from perspiration. I rubbed my hands over my cheeks and looked towards the baths where the boys were drying themselves off. I loathed myself and cursed my existence.

I was in need of distraction and was planning to have dinner with the geography master the following evening. Every time we met, I gave my new friend the benefit of my best brotherly advice. He was getting used to it. As the youngest of the masters, he had received advice from anyone who thought himself in a position to give advice, which was almost everyone. I thought we would go to the new hotel that had opened. I understood it had a fine barman who served a mixture of twenty-five cocktails to blow your head off. I would need that dead-head effect to endure my young friend's naïve platitudes.

I slipped into bed, too tired to read, too tired for anything. I fell asleep without even having to remember the last moment at which I was awake.

*   *   *

The weather was glorious. The morning birds gathered in a crescendo of applause. Ah, to have that perfect warm October day. England is seldom better. My hangover miraculously cleared, I leapt out of bed, an advertisement for good health. I avoided the half-empty bottle of whiskey and was down to the staff room with coffee in hand before all the boys had risen. I marked 2a's History test efficiently and generously, that suited my mood although Haycock's English really did give cause for concern; he writes like an ill-bred 'oik' from some industrial estate. The way he was going he would never pass his common entrance to Harrow. I made a vow that I would help him reach the standard to pass his entrance examination. The boy simply lacked belief and if I could galvanise his confidence, doubt would subside and he would not have to face failure at such a tender age. After the first lesson I took Haycock to one side and said, ' Do you mind if I have a word with you,' my new voice appearing out of nowhere, 'persevere young man, keep going, don't give up, you have the gift to be the best. I would have been grateful for five minutes to be someone like you at your age.' Whooops! A damn lie but I could see from his eyes that my words had installed an inner resolve.

'Thank you, sir,' he said, 'from now on I will try much harder.'

'I know you will,' I replied, 'and should you need any help or want any extra tuition, you just have to ask.' The boy left with a surprised smile that touched my heart and that, in truth, I found very moving.

The half hour morning break was spent either in a form room or in the echoing passageway where orange juice and milk was being served. On fine days such as these the boys were allowed to walk out onto the games field to catch some fresh air. Most had crowded outside to take some sun. I went in search of D to offer, or rather confide to him, that the part of Mortimer in the school play was his. At first I could not find him. I noticed the gym teacher Mister Cormack, showing off his muscles like a bloody whore playing an impromptu game of touch rugger with a sycophantic herd of juniors. His expression was as contrived as his posture, casting himself in a pose of lethargic arrogance.

D was returning from the far side of the field passing the music school, which looks nearer to completion by the day. He walked alone in the sun, the smell of summer well gone. A warm autumn mist was in the air. He was sucking his milk through a straw whilst humming a song rather loudly and doing both at the same time was no mean feat. I liked the fact that he was a loner, it reassured my conviction that he was a thinker, a boy of intelligence. He seemed startled by my call. 'I didn't mean to scare you,' I said. He did not answer.

'I would like you to play the lead role in the school play.'

He stood open-mouthed.

'I take that as a yes, a thank you, sir.'

'Thank you, sir,' he said, and hurtled back to his lessons.

I was happy that I could finally tell him. As I returned to my class I looked overhead and noticed a flock of seagulls flying towards the Norfolk coast. There, they would faithfully follow ships from Wells into the early part of their voyage until the remnants of meals were thrown overboard. Seagulls, I had been told, are the souls of dead sailors. And what, I wonder, happens to the souls of other mere mortals?

I had one free period before lunch so I returned to my room

to have a midday drink, a long drink. I could not remember who said: 'It is impossible to be both grateful and unhappy,' but during that hour it was certainly true, my mood had swung yet again. I sank onto my bed, stretched out my legs, put my hands behind my head and cradled my mind.

I knew in my heart that things were about to change. 'It's time to straighten yourself out Coles,' I said, 'barring a terrible accident, the future awaits.'

*   *   *

I chose to walk to dinner along the sea front. I had decided against the hotel idea and returned to the familiar Greek taverna. Since late afternoon my mood had shifted (precisely after finishing my double gin and tonic. I must remember that gin has a negative effect). I could not hold back certain thoughts, and was frightened that it was thought which distinguished man from animal; thought of conscience and thought of guilt. I lit a cigarette and welcomed the mix of tobacco and the sea air as my salvation. I chain-smoked until I reached the strip of bright red light bulbs illuminating the name *Aphrodite*. It stretched across the soulless street. What a greeting I thought. I am ravenous!

The geography master was waiting. The Greek owner welcomed me like a long lost brother, which was not surprising, as I seemed to be their only guest.

'Welcome to the handsome, Mr Coles,' the owner cheered, shaking my hand.

'Thank you, Demos. I am so glad to be back.'

I ordered a bottle of wine before I reached the table. 'Don't get up,' I said, 'Now where were we?' was my opening question. The geography master had the habit of pronouncing his vowels with suspicious care as he drank more and more wine. And as he became more intoxicated, his voice made obtuse sounds,

34

escaping vertically straight up to the sky. I leant over to catch a word. The way to listen to the geography master was to stand on his shoulders, from where you could see the first hint of baldness on the very top of his head. He complained a lot about his role at the school and felt he was not being challenged enough.

'Some more olives?' I asked, breaking up the tedium of his moan. How I wanted to tell him that there was something about him that reminded me of my life. And what may that be? I noticed some port that stood lonely on an empty dessert trolley. 'Port my good man,' I ordered, conjuring a smile and sounding as pleasant as possible. After it was poured I dismissed the two waiters as if dismissing two insubordinate boys from my study. The geography master took a good gulp and leant forward till the cheeks of his arse were on the very edge of his chair.

'I sometimes have disturbing dreams,' he admitted looking for a sign of recognition, an acknowledgement. But I did not respond and his face was transfixed like a rabbit in the headlights. Had he been too forward with his sharing? My smile splintered but the slight pause helped the geography master relax. I signalled the Greek patron.

'I do beg your pardon. Could we have some more port, Demos?' I asked in a quiet drawl whilst enjoying the hidden torment of my dinner companion.

'But my name is not Demos, Mr Coles.'

'Are you sure?,' I replied.

The geography master paid the bill and we walked back to the school along the main road. A car sped by with great speed. What matters is the pace be appropriate to one's mood. What do you think of that, Mister Geography teacher? A thing should go at the speed it goes or, as someone once said, 'Pace is God's style.' The driver had his right elbow slung outside the Jag's driver side window. Hair immaculate as moleskin, flashing teeth and hazel eyes, he was the son of the local industrialist, the local playboy flaunting his wears without a day's work behind him. I had seen him with his small nouveaux social group in the King George; a king buck among the nondescript rabbits.

I cursed out loud, 'Cunt!'

'What was that for?' asked the geography master.

'Frustration,' I replied, without thought.

*   *   *

The headmaster took me to one side.

'How is it going, Mr Coles?' he asked.

'Very well, headmaster . . . rehearsals are excellent . . . they all know their lines . . . I think we have a star in young D.'

He nodded, his face frowning as if he were instinctively suspicious, but then brightening up as I lied yet again about what a good choice of play it was. I should not be so uneasy or impatient when talking with him; not wise.

'We have some important visitors, VIP guests on the first night. Don't let us down,' were his parting words as he walked away uneasily as if balancing a tray full of glasses on one hand; surely the head had not been drinking?

He had disturbed my peace. I was irritated by his final Parthian shot. 'Don't let us down, Coles.' Bloody snob! I have met his type in all sorts of places. The type that always cleans the bath, wipes his feet on the mat the same number of times, gives up his seat to the elderly, and has never pissed in a swimming pool. The type that thinks he is invited to a party to make it go with a swing yet leaves alone at the end of the evening to an empty bed. If he ever decided to take his own life, he would make it look like an accident: 'Why, the poor fellow didn't know that the corner was so tight.'

My first impression of the headmaster was that he was a

ghastly bore. The second impression was the same. I have been and will be called many names in life, but 'boring' is not one of them . . . Nasty bastard, vile shit or pure evil maybe, but never a bore . . . that would be unforgivable!

As he disappeared from view, I fired my eyes, saying: 'If that's the way you want it, then that's the way you can fucking have it, but I warn you, don't ever utter the words "Don't let us down" again.' I have ways of dealing with suspicious sods, depending on the degree and nature of their distrust; in fact some of the ways can be rather painful using the most depraved instruments man has constructed.

*   *   *

I knew D would be a success. His shadow loomed over the insignificant play. One day he will perform to thousands and I will be recognised as the Svengali that first discovered his talent.

On the first day of rehearsals we had a read through. The cast sat either side of a table that had been set in the middle of the stage. I paced as the boys read out their lines. All rather hesitant except D who read with a fluency that gave me bumps all over my arms. I managed to stay cool, be calm; to know that this was a moment for that difficult thing called self-restraint. How I wanted to boast to the others, 'Listen to D, he's a natural.' But of course I didn't. Instead I clapped everyone for being superb and dismissed each with a thank you.

I retreated to my room with a slice of pride that I had least justified the casting of D. If anyone had the nerve to suggest favouritism in giving him the lead, I would simply say that all they needed to do was watch his performance. It should be said though without the tone of being defensive. We must not give away anything, not my secrets, my dark secrets . . . or my dark future.

Matron and her team had done a fine job with the costumes and make up. The boys dressed as the spinster aunts looked like the actresses in the movie *Little Women*. One in particular looked like a young Elizabeth Taylor – better keep an eye on him.

Frampton especially, with honey coloured hair and shy demeanour, played his part like a natural dame. How young boys love to dress up in women's clothes. As soon as they are set free of the tight ropes of their upbringing, they become liberated; I should encourage that search for freedom.

As I passed the library, the night before the opening, I saw a single light. All was silent except for the subdued murmur of a young voice repeating the same words. The soft glow from the bulb crept surreptitiously amongst the books. D's face bore a concentrated expression but evaporated into a sweet smile as I entered the library. He hastily looked away and continued his studying. It gave great comfort to see his dedication, the flush of attention. All this effort made just for me and my production.

I asked him if he was looking forward to the performance. He said he was. I asked if he knew his lines. He said that he knew 'each and every word'. I asked if his parents were coming down. He said they were and then curiously brought out a handwritten note from his father and showed it to me. He unfolded the blue writing paper. His dexterous movement was curiously beautiful. His brow wrinkled slightly as I read it, lips moist and smouldering. His hand stretched out for the note and I wanted to play a game of hide and seek under my jacket and hoped that he would fight to retrieve it. Reluctantly, I handed it over without a further word.

I sent him to bed quelling the emotion rising within me. 'Good luck tomorrow,' I might have said, but I don't remember. What I do remember is before he left, I touched his shoulder with a firm grip of affection. I could see surprise in his eyes but no more. He turned, shrugged, and sauntered away to his dormitory. I, in turn, felt tears fall from my tightly shut eyes, hearing the rain beat steadily down, and the sound of an imminent thunderstorm muttering beyond the horizon.

*   *   *

The morning of the opening night, I spent break inspecting the stage to see if everything was fine. Last year, in the middle of *If I were a Rich Man*, the Russian village collapsed; too much hilarity from the audience. I was not amused and promised this would not happen again.

I had decided against meeting the cast before they changed into costume. The dress rehearsal had gone to plan. Everyone knew their lines and I believed the production to be quite charming. In fact, I toasted its success with a furtive slug of my favourite tipple.

I had no afternoon lessons and was able to take a siesta for a good hour after marking a tedious quota of 2A History essays. For some reason I had lost all my red pens so had to mark with a pencil which I found had slipped by the side of the bed. It was blunt but I could not be fagged to walk down to the common room, so I sharpened it with a newly acquired steak knife; I remember stealing it from the kitchen to scrape off the tightly glued top from a whiskey bottle. The shavings from the pencil spattered the floor like earth into a grave. And it was at that exact moment that I had a feeling of foreboding. Where it came from I was unsure, but it was evident and I felt a presence signalling a warning. 'Oh God,' I thought and went for the Taylor's Port that I had been saving for a special occasion. I poured only two measures – not wanting to overdo it. Each was knocked back with a hearty swig and I felt better. I have got into the habit of giving myself marks out of ten for the state of my head. Before the slug of port minus three, after, a generous six; that was more like it.

I dressed in my almost new suit, the blue corduroy one. Nice white shirt properly ironed, and clean cuffs. I did not wear a tie as I wanted to give the air of a director. I switched on the electric heater and warmed my feet against it as a further form of relaxation. As I stared at my feet I realised I had odd socks on, so I looked into one of my drawers, and with a certain amount of difficulty, I found a fresh matching pair of navy blue. If I had to list my top ten tiresome chores, matching socks would be high up there. That small find raised my score to a seven. Before leaving my room I slapped my face with after-shave and swigged the half full bottle of scotch as a way to wish myself luck before replacing it on the shelf. As I walked down the stairs to face my public, I popped into my mouth two peppermint Polos as cover for the latest bout of drinking; probably a futile gesture but at least I had tried.

The library was rumbling with ordered commotion. Costumes being fitted and make up girls billing and cooing as they painted the boys' faces. Silly cows, the boys had hardly reached puberty. One, with a shrill voice, was particularly irritating. She was as common as muck, with small eyes hidden behind steel-rimmed glasses and her badly dyed hair hung below her shoulders. Nasty little whore she was and when I saw D's face, it was clear that he had too much make up on.

'Tone it down immediately,' I demanded, giving her a good ticking off, wanting in fact to say, 'leave him alone you nasty slag.' She started to remove some in a huff. As soon as I turned away she giggled and started to flirt with D and was about to make another comment when I was called out of the room by Mr Jeremy Lawrence, the newly acquired French teacher who was helping with the lights. What a strange chap he is, virile bass voice, clashing with a skeletal body. There is a campiness in the air wherever he walks and an unspoken philosophy of 'always be nice to someone you don't care about'. Thinking about it, perhaps I will steal that proverb. Anyway, I think the man is an oddball. I wouldn't trust him with any of my boys! I must ask the Geography master, another potential pervert, about him – must not forget now.

Lawrence needed a bulb to replace the one that was flickering on the stage table. At least he had noticed that before the opening call. I walked into the hall and to my delight it was packed. The school had to stand at the back, stacked so close they could read the dirt on each other's necks. And before I could wish my cast to 'break a leg', a hurried headmaster said we were running late and it was time for the curtain to rise.

I watched from the front row and readily admit it all went well, very well. Not the usual self-conscious performances – far from it – everyone performed most naturally and not a forgotten line between them. And, although I still believed it to be a rather silly play, it was the perfect tonic, more like a Dubonnet and soda than a vodka and orange, for evenings such as these. The headmaster profusely shook my hand afterwards, 'Bloody marvellous' he said, his eyes bright with pleasure. 'My wife adored it.'

'Well done, Mr Coles,' she enthused, wriggling her shoulders and digging her chin into her neck – looking like they were going to have their annual fuck that night.

D's father dressed in a two-buttoned navy blue suit and old Harrovian tie, lit a cigarette and removed a piece of tobacco from his lip. 'Can I ask the director to join us for dinner?'

I didn't hesitate, 'I will have to join you in an hour but thank you, I will be there.' I saw no sign of D's mother but I sensed it was not the time to ask; I knew, just knew that the thoughtless whore was gallivanting somewhere in London with her 'bit on the side' instead of seeing her beautiful son steal the show. Shame on her!

Father and son had already ordered when I arrived but I

41

wasn't too far behind. They had booked at Vincenti, the finest restaurant in town. Eight out of ten for food, four for atmosphere; but the low marks were not important, I was sitting with the finest company not just in Norfolk, but probably the whole of Britain. My glass was full of splendid Burgundy and it was good to discover that D's father, 'Call me John', had a penchant for drinking too. John poured the wine himself, sending the waiter away. He had fine hands, freshly manicured. They looked as if they had never done a day's labour. But he wouldn't would he, not his type?

We both praised D's performance and it warmed my heart to see the satisfaction glow from D's face. How special is he? Not for one instant did I sense anything but gratitude for the praise, not a hint of arrogance or smugness; so rare amongst his contemporaries believe me. I bad-mouthed Posey Major's performance just to hail D's even more, which was a bit shitty because Posey had been splendid. But who cares? As D ordered himself a vanilla ice cream, I was offered a large brandy. How civilised and my heart sang as the fine brandy poured into my mouth.

'Another?' John asked, making a gesture of tipping a glass towards the throat,

'Yes please, John.'

'Waiter' he ordered in the only way rich men can – a studied nonchalance, the click of a finger, 'A brandy for Mr Coles and the bill please.'

'But I can't drink alone, John,' I half-heartedly complained. But he had decided that he would return to London and discard the hotel room that he had booked. Oh, to be that wealthy and comfortable with life when you don't feel you should stay in a room just because you have booked it. He clearly had something on his mind, no doubt he wanted to rush back to check that absent wife. I wanted to say, 'If you need to share anything old boy, I am a good listener.' But it was too early for that sort of over familiarity; the time would surely come. I waited by the car as D said his farewell. The street was as silent as a morgue and standing on the other side of the road I could hear John's praise being bestowed upon his son.

As D left his father and walked to my car, my heart began to beat faster and my head began to whirl. Instinctively, I shouted at the boy to stop dawdling and I could see from his expression that my sudden change of tone made him wonder. Surely he is beginning to recognise my emotional turmoil. I have noticed an attitude with his friends, that aloofness. 'Come and have a game of football?' they would ask and he would walk away without a word, making the other boys act perplexed.

By the time we reached the school gates, my mood lightened and before he left the car I congratulated him for all his dedicated hard work on the role; he said, thank you, 'Thank you', softly and I think he was about to stroke my hand in gratitude for the recognition but resisted. 'Good-night, sir, see you tomorrow.'

'Good night fair child.'

I spent the rest of the evening flat on my bed, bottle in hand. The hammer of thunder from the drink, and there D slept not far from where I lay.

I stared at my favourite picture and debated the justification for befriending my pupils. I thought of the future, of when I would be headmaster and how I would recruit with a blind eye the occasional master with my proclivities. I felt like an S.S. officer, having a nose for the hidden Jew. I would easily be able to detect the pervert in our midst. Lawrence for one would never be allowed to settle.

'God help me!' I shouted out loud, for a moment thinking I had awoken the whole school. It might have been true that my tolerance had soared and that I was beginning to learn how to wait, to love, and to live and let live, but it was also true that after nights such as these my hunger for D was leaving me angry, lonely and tired.

*   *   *

The early morning breeze was cold and flapped the curtains. I leant my head out of the window to greet it and to ease the touch of delirium tremens; two out of ten. I sat on the edge of my bed and waited for the room to come back to its senses. I looked at my watch; my God it was a minute past five a.m. I am going to wake D. I found myself creeping up the stairs, along the corridor after pouring the near empty bottle of whiskey into my mouth. I tip toed along the wooden floorboards, creaks rattling against my nerves. *Shush, be quiet!*

The dormitory slept soundly. D's bed was the second along on the far side. I sat at the end. His tartan cover had slipped on the floor and I picked it up and placed it back on top of his body. I leant forward. I could hear the sound of his breath – breathing strongly through his nose. 'I just want to congratulate you on your performance. You acted like the star I know you are. I am so proud of you – you beautiful, beautiful creature.' I heard Proudlock who was asleep in the next bed, let out a huge yawn. His movement startled me and I snapped out of my drunken daze. Where is your discipline Mr Coles? I rose slowly and sneaked back to my room. I don't believe Proudlock heard anything, even if a funnel from a cruise ship had bellowed he would not have stirred.

I went back to bed hoping to catch up on some lost sleep. Instead, I stayed awake; eyes wide open with that delicious tingle in the head that usually comes from the perfect blend of peace of mind and a slight current of fresh air.

*   *   *

44

The headmaster and his wife gave me a dinner tonight; a way of thanking me for all my hard work and success with the school play. 'Such a wonderful play,' Mrs Draper said a dozen times if she said it once, adding, 'I loved the film you know.'

We were served avocado with prawns followed by steak. The dinner was easy and, surprisingly, I enjoyed it. I had gone expecting much worse, as if visiting the dentist for the first time and dreading the pain of a filling. But conversation over dinner remained calm even though the suspicion that the dentist would suddenly, without warning, tilt back the head and take out all the teeth one by one, loomed like an uninvited guest.

The head's dining room was so tidy. I hardly dare pick up the knife and fork because I did not want to spoil the perfect arrangements. After dinner we were led into the drawing room. I remained standing so I did not poach the head's favourite chair. When the head went out to fetch his favourite Port, which seemed to be fast becoming my preferred drink, Mrs Draper bustled around straightening pillows that were already straight and insisting that I sit down. There was a rumour that she was on an intense diet but the loss of a few extra pounds were not evident; her life was one of struggle between greed and vanity. She had dragged the fight on for years but neither side had a chance of winning, like boxers each vowing to fight to the death but neither finding that knock-out punch. She was never going to return to the slim lass that the head had first seen at Chester Races – he had told me about their meeting at our dinner two days after I had arrived at the school. I thought for a moment that she had a fancy for me but I could not stand that contemplation and felt a heave in my stomach.

Matron, who was invited to make up the numbers, always looked at me with that threat of 'cod liver oil for you my lad'. She had the fucking annoying habit of calling me Clifford, being probably the only one in the school or outside to be so familiar. It has always been Coles and always will be Coles – silly cow!

'Clifford, can I pass you some more port?'

No thank you, you fucking shrew – not from that dragon's claw. I glided a knife into her eye socket. Ah, the joy of that, the sublime satisfaction . . .

'Yes please, matron!' I replied like a prick.

'What are you planning for us next year, Clifford?'

'Planning? What do you mean, matron, or can I call you Doris?'

'Matron will do Clifford thank you . . . What play do you plan to direct for us mere mortals next year, silly?'

'Well the choice is not mine. Mrs Draper came up with a winner this year, so I bow down to her expertise,' smiling at the headmaster's wife and quietly laughing so much that I nearly coughed into my drink.

The headmaster went on and on and on about the primary and secondary school education in the country. Dull would be kind. I was drowning in boredom, the foaming froth of its sea reaching my neck. There was no room for questions, no opportunity to change the subject. I think I was nodding off just as Mrs Draper asked, 'One more drink, Mr Coles?'

'No thank you, Mrs Draper.'

'Well life is full of surprises . . . coffee then?'

'Thank you, Mrs Draper,' my voice suddenly going into a minor key.

'You should join me for one of my morning jogs, Mr Coles.'

I retched slightly at the thought of it. 'Thank you Mrs Draper. That sounds . . . um . . . bloody wonderful.'

I comforted myself with the fact that this charm initiative would gain my promotion.

'Head of History, Coles?'

'Thank you, headmaster.'

I stood to say my goodbyes a little after eleven o'clock. My thanks were enthusiastic but not over done like the beef. 'The finest dinner, sir, I have had for years, the wine was sublime.' Ha!

When I looked at the mirror on my return, I saw an overweight ogre. Perhaps it was my contemplation about weight earlier in the evening that made me think I was heavier than I actually was. I was beginning to look ugly. Perhaps my own fight between vanity and greed was about to begin or already had without notice. I did not drink any more that evening which was a minor miracle, perhaps due to the fact that all I had left in the cabinet was a lonesome 'Special Brew' beer. I thought about the night before and decided that my infatuation with D should calm. I dealt with it last night like an overzealous drunk. If I am to behave like that, I must be more composed. Yes, maybe some drink inside but never too much.

*   *   *

The play was coming to the end of its short run. It was beginning to take up too much of my time. What time you may ask? I am a teacher with responsibilities. What time? 'The time for proper conscientious work,' I say.

I had a sherry in the common room and promised myself that from tonight I would start living a full life in this godforsaken town. I felt a frisson of foreboding when things were going well. I also felt I was getting old, portly, and bored. I slammed down another sherry but it made little difference, I was flat.

D had his mother in the audience for the final night. She patted her son on the head as a way of congratulations for his performance. She was over-polite and somewhat cold, I had the sense that she didn't particularly like me or perhaps it was simply distrust. She acted somewhat disapprovingly but I played it straight and was very charming. I was half, or should we say, three quarters expecting to be invited to dinner but she had to hurry back to London, probably to get to some glamorous, vacuous party. I noticed regret on D's face but he acted bravely and hid as best he could his deep disappointment.

'See me to my car darling,' she said, and he followed her out. She did not offer a goodbye or congratulation for a wonderful evening. Never mind, she will soon get to know me better – that I promise.

I peeled off to say hello to the other parents who had sauntered backstage to be with their children. Jempson, who played Teddy, introduced his mother and father for a third time in as many days. They asked whether I would like to join them for dinner. I politely refused. It was bound to be fearfully boring. They were heading off to the awful Indian, the rather aptly named Khyber Pass, which pompously boasts on its window as being the finest Indian restaurant in Norfolk. I ate there once and the only good thing I could critique was an hour after I left, I felt as if I had lost an extraordinary amount of weight. Jempson's father is a magistrate and old boy of the school. The minute he opened his mouth he got on my nerves. He had a querulous tone and mentioned Eton and Cambridge at least five times in our five-minute conversation. No thank you, I preferred my own company.

Just before I made a hasty retreat to my room, the boy Jempson knocked hard on the table. 'Quiet please,' he shouted, 'Mr Coles, sir; we would like to present you a gift from the entire cast for the kindness you have shown during this production. You have given us . . . the best ever time we have had at this school.' He handed over a book-sized parcel. 'May I?' I asked and unwrapped the brown paper to reveal . . . a book on the life of Charles Dickens.

'Three cheers for Mr Coles!' cried D who had returned from saying goodbye to his mother. 'Hip hip hooray, hip hip hooray, hip hip hooray!' It was the perfect scene. I was surprised, shocked, gobsmacked.

'Boys,' I said, 'to receive this recognition from you, is probably my finest hour . . . thank you.' I mouthed a final 'thank you' to D. It may have been inappropriate but no one noticed. Although I had read in a local rag the previous week that mouthing a thank you can look as if you're saying 'I love you.'

I crept from the room and noticed my heart pounding and shirt damp with sweat. I stripped down to my underpants and let out a chuckle and closed the curtains. It was time for my very own private celebration; I opened up a fresh bottle and started to drink; a beautiful bottle of Irish whiskey, single malt. The brand of Knappogue Castle was written in celtic font on its label. I had kept it safe for a night such as this. I was so thirsty that my head was saying 'drink it up, drink it up'. And I did, quickly and without thought. Not the whole bottle mind you, a little over half. As I shoved the bottle across my desk, I decided that I would go for a walk to get some air. I tucked in my shirt, straightened my tie, and stepped into the chilly corridor; Proudlock was passing my door, going for a pee.

'Where are you off to, Proudlock?'

'I needed to go the toilet, sir.'

'Well hurry back to bed afterwards.'

'I will, sir . . . and, sir?'

'Yes, Proudlock?'

'I thought the play was fantastic tonight.'

I did not answer but instead decided against the walk and returned to my room to have another drink.

It was very nearly the perfect day.

*   *   *

'Sir, will you help us decorate the classroom?'

The boys had the special privilege of plastering their class-rooms with ghastly Christmas decorations during the last week of winter term.

'Of course, boys,' I replied to my History class. I could not think of anything worse but my status was soaring and I wasn't about to blow my new-found popularity which shhh, don't tell anyone, but I was enjoying. I could hear the boys saying over their Christmas lunch, 'Mr Coles is such a fantastic teacher, he is our absolute fave!' I have made another note though that when I am headmaster, there will be none of this Christmas cheer.

The mornings were dark. The sea air was becoming too intimate, and a veil of mist hovered over the school grounds. It made the last days of the winter term so sluggish. The damp weather waterlogged the grounds and the last week of rugby was cancelled. This did not help the mood of the school. The boys were restless and in search of some fun. On the last Saturday, *It's a Wonderful Life* was shown – a dreary choice from a dreary lady. Mrs Draper proudly cooed, telling anyone who listened that it was her mum's favourite. Masters were invited to watch the film.

'Good for morale, if the boys see the masters joining in the fun,' the headmaster advised at the last staff meeting of term. But not for me, headmaster. I have had enough of crawling up your ass. I was beginning to feel as if I was being blindfolded and only catching a glimpse of an imagined figure before I crashed into it. I needed air and as the first frame glowed, I sneaked out escaping onto the first XV pitch and sat on the single bench dressed in a heavy coat, my blue scarf wrapped round my throat. I took out a cigarette, tapped the end on the wooden arm, lit up and began to smoke in search of peace until I was startled by a gust of wind that shook the rugby posts. Did

I hear the voice of impending doom, a heavy burst of tut tutting? No, it was only my conscience.

I was about to throw my cigarette butt to the ground when I heard footsteps. Can't anyone get some peace round here? I peered into the gloom. Although I heard a mumbled voice, a face was, I swear, not there. And I wondered whether it was my imagination that conjured up the outline of a skull, deep pits of eyes and rank upon rank of teeth . . .

Slowly the geography master appeared in focus.

'I need to have a word,' he said.

I wanted to get rid of him immediately but saw he had a flask in hand and so I moved along the bench to make room.

'Yes?'

He had a bleak and macabre expression. Oh dear I thought, we can't have this conversation here. I suggested, or was it that I ordered the geography master to follow me to the local bar. It had recently reopened to huge suburban fanfare a half mile down the road.

'But shouldn't we watch the end of the film?' he asked lamely, his face looking far younger than his twenty-five years.

'Absolutely not,' I replied. 'We are not on duty and really you must stop trying to ingratiate yourself with the headmaster. It is so pitiful to watch.'

The newly decorated bar struck me at once as a potential den of provincial iniquity. There were low lights and plenty of scope for gin and flirtation. The bar stools were occupied with eager-to-please regulars and alcoves in which the lonely could slink away with their resentment. The landlord was over familiar and efficient; he opened our wine at the table.

'From the local school are we?' he enquired in an irritatingly contrived jovial tone.

'If you mean Falston, the answer is yes.' I dismissed him with a shrug. I am not going to have Falston ever be known as the 'local' school. That would not do, I mean there was a comprehensive down the road.

'Do we look that obvious?' the geography master asked.

'You do,' I replied. Here he was, our geography master in an ill-fitting tweed suit, leatherette elbow patches and too much oil on his swept back hair.

'I have to talk to you about something, Coles – I am sure you will be able to point me in the right direction – to guide me so to speak.' He was stammering away, flustered and uneasy with himself. 'I have terrible thoughts just below the surface that I am having a struggle to contain.'

I bit my lower lip so as not to smile.

'Below the surface?' I muttered and then added icily, 'There is no surface, it is either there or it is not.' I was pointing to my head, jab jab jab. 'Don't deny it, live with it.' I enjoyed watching him squirm. I was not prepared to have a debate on the matter. The geography master was down. If I had any advice it would be to remain still; using a boxing expression, 'Stay on the canvas a little longer.' The fighter that gets up too quickly after being knocked down only reveals that he is badly hurt. 'If you wish to confess something, then we can make believe a confessional grill, here, between us and I will be all ears – another drink?'

But before I could get up he started to lambast the headmaster. 'He is a charlatan, bloody useless third-rate head,' the bitterness bucketed from his mouth. When someone starts talking shittily to me about someone else, I am at once suspicious that they could and probably would do the same to me. 'Another drink . . . ?'

I skipped the landlord's offer of another bottle of wine and went for two generous, 'make it a treble' brandies. The landlord poured the cognac into balloon glasses and when he handed mine over I held it to the light and saw an odd mist descending into the caramel liquor.

'And what's this?' I asked rhetorically.

'It's Hobson's choice,' he answered with a sick half-grin of someone well satisfied with himself, as if he had just learnt the expression from a local newspaper.

I had noticed recently that strangers tried consistently to have the upper hand in short exchanges. The landlord and I would never have a comfortable exchange even if I came into his bar a hundred times. I am sure, that as I returned to the table, I heard him mutter, 'We don't want your sort here.' The voice seemed so clear that I glanced back over my shoulder. He was however at the other end of the bar serving someone else. How odd, those voices seem to be getting louder and louder.

'Now where were we?'

The geography master had taken a cigarette from my Rothman's pack and was puffing away. As he inhaled long and deep, it seemed as if his face had gone numb. It gave the impression that he had already said too much. An unfair quotation came to mind: 'He hasn't an enemy in the world and none of his friends like him!' The poor man was so alone, alone with his demons. Why did he choose me to confess his darkest thoughts?

I wasn't in the mood to be his confessor. Pray to God, I should advise him to get down on his jellied knees, weep for forgiveness, and live a life of abstinence, as that would be his one chance for salvation. But I kept these words to myself. In fact, I found it reassuring that there was someone, more tortured than I, in our midst.

*   *   *

The term had been beneficial overall: mentally, possibly; emotionally, probably; spiritually: certainly. Well, perhaps I am lying a little – but with Christmas looming I was allowed to give myself an encouraging end of term report.

For the Carol Service, D had been chosen to be the soloist for *Away in a Manger;* an unexceptional honour for the boy with the finest voice in school.

The hall was crammed with an over-enthusiastic mob of parents jostling to get the best seat. As the service began, the fathers seemed to sway in synchrony whilst salivating over a junior boy's blonde mother sitting cross-legged in the front row. I had a longing to get out of there as soon as D had sung. How ugly these parents were; yet I should remember that almost anything is ugly in the wrong mood.

I noticed that D's mother had not bothered to attend. His father was of course standing proud, camera in hand, waiting for the perfect snap of his son in a single-breasted red hassock. A double click and snap went the camera.

D performed with a beauty rarely found in someone so young. His mouth slowly sang each word, showing the tip of his tongue as he tackled each vowel. There was no sign of nerves, just a confident young man stepping into the light and showing us all what a talent he truly is. I wanted to stand and applaud as the final line was sung but instead I turned my head away to hide my own smile; there was no applause during the service except of course after the headmaster's 'We have had a jolly good term and have a Happy Christmas' speech.

The boys stood up to leave the service a second too early, which caused a ripple of 'Oh dear' from masters. But who can blame them, the modern materialistic seduction of Christmas was upon us and in comparison the winter term must have seemed very dull.

'Thank you for all you have done this term Mr Coles.' D's father offered his beautifully manicured soft hand. 'The boy thinks a lot of you.'

D was pushing his trunk into the boot of the car. The background noise of howling and yelling began to diminish as the cars drove away. I set my falling eyes on the boy for the last time that year as he finally managed to pack everything away.

'It was my pleasure, John. He is a very good student.'

'Come and say goodbye to Mr Coles and thank him.' D came over and offered his hand. 'Thank you, sir,' his handshake stronger than ever before.

Was that a long face I saw when he offered his hand, a sense of loss? Probably not, more like 'Goodbye, sir, I must go!' I will not kid myself when it comes to interpreting D's mood.

Their silver Bentley headed out of view and back to London. I wondered if it wasn't once blue. Ah such wealth, such breeding. Finally the driveway in front of the school was empty. The noise had evaporated and there was suddenly nothing. Nothing and no one, except the wind and three bloated seagulls flying directly above. I felt quite lonely. I was on my own again to face the days and the weeks ahead. I was reluctant to move, as if moving from where I stood would break the spell of the now, previous term – ridiculous really.

*　　*　　*

It was a week later that I was reading and feeling content with my own company. The school was empty except for the occasional whistle from the irritating Portuguese charladies. I was scratching my scalp until dandruff fell to my chair when I heard an enticing knock on my door. Could a single man be so very wrong?

'Who is there on this dark night?' I answered. Mrs Draper, that was who, with bottle of wine in one hand and a sense of anger in the other. She had some right to be angry. She had, after all, been living with the headmaster for ten years. The drain on even her ample resources must have been agonising.

'I understand you are heading off tomorrow for the Christmas break,' she emitted with a deep breath. If that means visiting my sister and her dreary family for some Christmas cheer – the answer was yes.

Her eyes darted all around the room like lizard's eyes. She looked at the picture of the figure on the wall. She mumbled how exotic it was and took a sip of the cheap wine that she had opened and then poured. 'I go spare in this bloody school when the boys have left for their holiday; so cold, so empty don't you find Mr Coles? Don't you miss the boys?' She put her hand on my knee to offer a little sympathy.

I nodded and removed her hand. I did not like her tone, her voice was grating and the constant licking of her lips was even more reptilian. She had picked up a book of poetry and wiping off the dust, she started to read out loud. Was it by chance or was it by choice that she chose Goethe's *Ganymede*:

> How, in the morning brightness,
> You all around shine at me,
> Springtime, Beloved!
> With thousandfold love-bliss
> The holy feeling
> Of your eternal warmth
> Presses itself upon my heart,
> Unending beauty!
>
> Could I but embrace you
> In this arm!
>
> Ah, upon your breast
> I lie, languish,
> And your blossoms, your grass
> Press upon my heart.
> You cool the burning
> Thirst of my bosom,
> Lovely morning-wind!

There calls the nightingale
Lovingly for me from the misty vale

I come, I come!
Whither, ah whither?

Up! Up it surges.
The clouds are leaning
Downwards, the clouds
Bow down to yearning love.
To me! To me!
In your lap, clouds,
Upwards!
Embracing, embraced!
Upwards to thy bosom,
All-loving Father!

She lowered the book and looked at me.

What was that? A slight breeze gently flapped the curtains, the window was open, and apparently of its own accord. I went to close it. Damn cold, the weather was that week. My head had begun to spin due to the roughest plonk I had drunk for years. 'Brandy?' I asked, trying to regain my senses. I did not wait for an answer before I had slugged two mouthfuls down. Unfortunately it did not help and I had to sit down to take in deep breaths. My stomach had its first lurch of the week. I was thinking of lying down on the floor and pretending to be dead but thought that would not work.

'Let me make you some tea,' Mrs Draper offered. She knew just how to kick a man when he was down.

'No you should go,' but she would not listen.

'Do you ever think how many of your dreams have come true, Mr Coles?' She emptied the kettle and rinsed out the lime scale. I did not answer, 'and how many promises you have kept?'

Again I did not answer. And before my very eyes I hallucinated that she turned into a toad that I was treading on with that horrible sensation of texture.

'What about some fresh air? You suddenly look a little peaky.' Mrs Draper reopened the window that I had only just closed. 'That's it, take in deep breaths.' From the corner of my eye I saw her bend down to pile more logs on my sorry fire. I felt as if Mrs Draper was leading me into a voyage of strange and complicated events; I was not wrong.

'Shall we have sex?' She asked without warning, her face a map of anticipation. I felt no compunction to say yes or to say no. I simply needed to support myself against the wall as I was about to lose my balance. There is nothing worse than being in a lousy physical state, especially when you feel unable to take the necessary steps to do anything about it. I couldn't think straight – not even of England. Mrs Draper opened her mouth or was it a smile? With the sweep of an arm more masculine than mine, she dragged me towards her face, knocking over the dregs of my tea and started to kiss my mouth voraciously like a trollop in one of those John Wayne movies.

'Oh dear God,' I grumbled, a demonic ring of bells going off loudly in my head. I fumbled around like a lost child in the dark. Soon we were humping on my bed in that non-fuss slow motion way. Where was my stamina? The smell of her body resembled the stench of cooked chicken carcass, her skin as white as uncooked tripe. I swayed, cursed, and coughed. Afterwards I pushed her away like a child does to a plate of unwanted food. My immediate thought surprised me; one of self-pity.

'I better hurry now, the headmaster may be wondering where I am.' She was lowering her dress, an adulterer with happy eyes and huge teeth. 'If I don't see you before you head off . . . Have a wonderful Christmas, Clifford.' She left my room but not before offering her hand to shake. 'Oh yes, happy New Year!' We had returned to our former selves.

Instinctively I grabbed for a handkerchief and stuffed it into my mouth believing I was about wrench my guts out. It was definitely time to head to London and give myself a damn good talking to over my general behaviour. 'He could do better,' my newly rewritten report would have to say. Before I fell asleep with fire burning and glass in hand, I did have a moment of panic that Mrs Draper went back and told her husband what had just happened. 'Really, Mr Coles, you really should not go round fucking my wife.'

'But, headmaster, I would never fall to such a degree of human banality. I would never do something so mundane – you can ask any of the boys that.'

*   *   *

The following morning I greeted the day as if struck by a belt. I quickly had a shower to rid myself of any human residue, followed by a shave. I splashed cologne over my face to mask my hangover. I packed my bag and crept out of my door, closing it quietly and double locking with my silver key, which I placed into my top pocket. I certainly didn't want to bump into anyone. I tip-toed surreptitiously from the grounds and crept through the cold streets to the station.

The restaurant was quiet, lit by a blinding December sunlight. It was crisp and stark inside. There was none of the usual bustle of those waiting for the early Norwich train. I ordered two sausages, eggs, buttered toast and black coffee to fill the warmth inside, with a copy of *The Times* to read on the train. The 7.30am was punctual and I found a seat without any difficulty. It jerked out of Cromer station, halted ten minutes down the track and pulled away into the backwaters of England. I glanced out of the moving train and caught sight of football pitches, waterlogged fields, and cows standing in rows under trees. I started to read my paper but couldn't reach the end of the front page without the feeling that I was being watched. A woman with flowing black hair and dark brown eyes gazed straight through me. She had a face that seemed to belong to another era. The time of pretty parasols, trams on the beachfront, donkey rides and candy floss. There was an uncanny silence followed by a soft muttering coming from her direction. I was not sure what was being said but it sounded like an offering, a sense of prayer. I smiled, gave a gentle nod of acknowledgement. She smiled back. Her mouth opened to reveal broken teeth and her halitosis nearly struck me down.

'You are going to Hell!' She said in a deep manly voice. What did she say? She moved her tongue slowly around her mouth like a lizard dying in the sun. Damn woman, should we meet again I might find her talking to the nearest lamppost.

The memory of the previous night suddenly revisited. I sullenly rose and tried to walk calmly. I had an urge to vomit. A ticket inspector approached, limp-wristed, a lisping sort of prototype conveniently adopted by homophobes as an example of what Humanity can become if virile standards are not maintained, if not indeed enforced.

'Ticket please,' he said. I noticed I had goose pimples and bumps over my arm as I handed it over. The train shunted and drew to a sudden stop. I had no time to take the ticket back; instead I ran, holding my hand to my mouth, and swallowing back the vomit.

The toilet whiffed of urine; the window was jammed, unable to open. I glimpsed myself in the mirror and heaved into the sink. The luminosity of my skin was mesmerising. I could not stop staring at the fluidity of the pigmentation. There was no colour, just the merciless clarity of the body exposed from human emotion; it must have been a frightening sight to all those who could see me. I cursed my health and bowed my head. The train's engine sounded the last post as I splashed the tepid water onto my face for salvation.

When I returned to my seat, a long hour after I had made my sudden exit, the compartment was empty; there was no sign of anyone. Perhaps it had been the mere sight of me; they probably had hurried off at the previous stop in disgust.

I changed at Norwich and caught the London train. It shuffled all the way to Liverpool Street Station. I walked gingerly along the platform, a pace appropriate to my mood. I needed a drink and a ham sandwich, something of substance inside. The bar was in the far corner, a red neon sign flashing 'Prince Albert' above the door. It was a tomb of a place, a coffin for mad poets.

'A whisky please and one of those sandwiches?'

The drink ignited a fire in my guts and a discharge of vomit to my larynx. The sandwich that followed calmed everything down. I went to the cigarette machine to buy twenty Rothmans. Silence again. My mind retreated, and I sat with no thought of the coming hours. But then I felt exhausted, as if I had run a cross-country race. 'One more, please, barman and I'm off.'

'Have this one on the house.' The barman's offer surprised and even touched me.

I apologised for my sallow complexion and the state I was in. I heard birds pass overhead like angels of death. I needed to get out. Enough! It was time for me to move on like a sensible rat or like a vulture anticipating more deaths ahead.

I could not deal with my sister when I felt like this. She would shake her head and mumble that I had been drinking again, saying sarcastically, 'My, you do look well, Clifford.' I needed a rest, time to regain my strength and time to drain the alcohol. I noticed a bed and breakfast just across the road.

'A room please.'

The concierge said nothing, simply pointed at the cost per night pinned to the wall.

He handed over the key, which had been lying in his lap.

'Not even a number?' I said, trying to lighten his mood and in fact, mine.

'First door on the right,' he said, finally opening his mouth.

The room was cold and the radiator long dead. I felt a chill go through my body. My teeth were chattering, like skeleton bones or xylophone keys – yes, skeletons playing xylophones. I wanted to eradicate everything from my mind; to find some calm, calm, calm . . .

I scratched my neck and then slumped onto the bed acknowledging the fact that doubt, fear, hate, probably all negative feeling, is sometimes the result of being sick, incapable of facing oneself and therefore obliged to drink more and more, becoming sicker and sicker, and sicker and sicker, as if trapped on another jerking carousel.

I needed to sleep and looked down at the miserable bed. I found an extra blanket at the bottom of the single closet standing unevenly in the corner. I caught myself taking a look, in case anyone was hiding there, lurking and listening. With a coat on and two blankets, I still felt the cold and the sodding noise out on the street. It was touching my nerve ends, as a pneumatic drill might disturb that poor person with his first chance of a lie-in for a year, or like that alcoholic dentist prodding at the teeth with his probe before he has had sufficient drink to calm his nerves. I closed my eyes but soon realised that was no chance of a morning sleep. CANT THEY STOP THAT FUCKING NOISE?

I returned to the roars of the city and to the rush of myself coming to. I procrastinated about whether to take the subway to my sisters or to catch the nicer, warmer – but more expensive option – the black cab. How many times have we procrastinated for so long that by the time we take action, the original reason for that action has evaporated? The minutes of delicious indolence mounted until I shouted out, 'TAXI!'

'Could you take me to suburban London, to the village of Wimbledon?' The house of my parents, the house of my birth, the house of horrors.

'Lovely day,' the taxi driver yelled, all jovial over the Christmas traffic. Then we stood in a traffic jam, the driver giving the hoot, joining in the excitement with the rest of the Christmas revellers. All hoots, gesticulations. 'Christ it is snowing. Get a bloody move on.'

I noticed I had trodden in a big dog turd just as I was about to enter the cab and it was beginning to stink. Not such a lovely day now Mister 'Oh I am so cheerful' driver, Mister Cabbie.

'Pull over here at No 23.'

He turned his wheel in an exaggerated manner.

'How much?'

God you are raking it in! I handed over the exact fare. No tip for him, no Christmas cheer from this passenger.

The cab driver began to rant about the smell and my meanness. I turned and spat – the globule slipped slowly down his windscreen; I strode away not looking back. It was quite unlike my usual behaviour, but a psychologist would probably diagnose: 'He was heading to the home of his pre-pubescent years and fearful of the fact.' If it had taken the driver that long for the gentle whiff of shit to reach his nose, it may take a similar time for him to notice the phlegm? But it did not. He got out of his cab, hands gesturing obscene signs and yelled 'Wanker!' But instead of chasing me, he took the fare of an elderly woman who looked unsteady under feet. 'Can I help you ma'am?' His hand turned from a V-sign to the hand of care and support. Good sort after all, English to the core. The last I saw of him, he was on his knees dusting, spitting, and polishing the back seat with the elderly lady holding her nose.

*   *   *

The door was ajar but I still knocked, knocked, knocked; my timing was getting better. I am not one of those who will knock and walk in whether the door is answered or not.

My nephew, Sean Claude Friday, greeted me with, 'Hello, Uncle Clifford.' He is polite and quite charming, the only son of Donald Friday and my sister Jean. Donald, a forty-year-old dour Lancastrian slob with his stomach overflowing his belt, works as an executive at Moss Bros.

I was led into the suburban kitchen, still the tone of polished grey, the colour of my youth. The large central table was set for tea with cups and saucers and a collection of colourful party cakes placed neatly on a blue plate. My dear tidy, ordered sister, looking so bored, so predictable.

'Hello ,Clifford, my, you do look . . . well,' she lied and gave me a little kiss on the cheek. Oh for the grace of patience!

She looked straight into my eyes and was about to add something but was distracted and turned away. That was how it has always been; on the verge of confiding a secret, a word of advice, an observation, but then silence.

My dear sister was perceived to be dull. Without compunction, she had the habit of bringing out holiday snaps of her son. I had learnt not to show too much enthusiasm in case the previous year's photos were brought out as well.

The house still looked very much the same as when I was growing up; a collection of dentist waiting-rooms. Few guests invited, not a cushion out of place, shelves packed with old books that I had once devoured and varied knick-knacks from obscure European towns. The house was bestowed to us

64

grudgingly in Father's will. I walked around it as if wearing dark glasses, every room growing darker as though a storm was about to break. I screamed in horror that one day I might continue to live there.

'Make me an offer, Jean, for my share, and it is yours,' I started my negotiation. It was like talking to someone blind, yet whose eyes seemed to look straight at you, even into and through. But enough of the psycho-babble 'You have a deal, Jean, and may you live happily ever after in this house of horror, forever more.'

Donald arrived home at the stroke of six o'clock wearing what looked like a Moss Bros suit. 'Clifford is in the lounge dear, pour him a drink would you?' Jean shouted twenty feet up from the first floor landing.

No need, Donald, I have a sherry in hand.

'Do you mind?' he said, as he poured himself a large gin and tonic and then slurped it with his pomegranate lips.

'You are lucky not having to travel to work, Clifford; London Transport, please . . . '

'All that commuting should be good for the figure,' I replied, tapping my stomach but he didn't take the bait, instead he crashed onto the sofa and let out an exaggerated heave. He talked about his work (yawn), how weddings were as popular as ever (yawn), not once meeting my eye as if he was in a prison line-up and didn't want to give away his identity. The drone of his voice, the drone of trivia, made me want to heave. I was consumed with despair and boredom, suffocation, even suicide and/or murder. It was a relief when my sister called to say that young Sean would like ME to read him a bedtime story. I virtually sprinted upstairs to the room that once was mine. Not that different, perhaps even the same bed and sea green armchair.

My nephew sat with arms crossed, bottom lip hanging down

to chin. I sat beside and heard his breath, slightly nasally. 'Blow your nose boy,' I thought, but said nothing and instead read an Irish fable about greed and leprechauns.

'Please finish the story, uncle.' The boy played on my emotions and gently I surrendered and read to the last word of the predictable tale. He looked up and let out a yawn.

'Shall I keep the door open?' I asked.

'No, please close it, I don't want any light,' and for a moment I was moved, touched even, by a memory that was not so distant after all. 'Good-night then.'

*   *   *

'Don't you want your dinner?' my sister asked.

'Just off to the pub . . . and alone,' a touch of genuine anger crept into my voice. Anger, matched with the house, went neatly together . . . with tiredness . . . with loneliness . . . with despair.

Wimbledon High Street was littered with smiles, self-importance and light jackets, even though the temperature had dropped to a deep chill. The pub was full of judges, magistrates, bankers and even teachers. I asked for my favourite tipple and the barman poured a double, smiling as if in an advert for cereal. For a moment there was silence all around, people staring but then they started to talk again – slowly at first, then ordinarily, then extraordinarily. There was a buzz of inquisitiveness. Were they truly talking about me? They seemed to be asking a question. I was very keen to know what the question was.

'And how are you?' a young man standing to my left asked.

I looked blankly.

'Is that the question?'

'Yes.' He replied without hesitation.

He was copper-skinned with greasy slicked black hair; yet another foreigner. I bought the greasy one a drink. He took it without thanks.

'I suppose you have completely forgotten about such ordinary things as good manners, gratitude, conviviality, friendship, dare I say, love or ordinary words such as YES, PLEASE, NO AND THANKS.' I was the one now short of breath, indeed I felt like a pearl diver who had stayed down too long. I needed another drink to calm my nerves, the tremors had begun, the shake of the hand and a hint of sweat on the brow. Damn it! My head drooped and it was then that the lad took pity and remarked on my distress.

'I need some fresh air,' I pleaded into his ear and the foreigner jumped from his stool, 'My English no good,' he said but seemed to understand my plea. He helped me out like a caretaker for an elderly relative. The cold air gave back my balance. I asked him if he wanted to walk. He did not answer. I then noticed how beautiful he was; so beautiful was he, as John Keats once wrote, and scores of corny reporters ever since, 'Truth is beauty and beauty is truth; that is all you know, all you ever need to know.' I told him how extraordinary he was and my churlish and shaky mood suddenly evaporated.

'Shall we go for a walk?'

'Yes please, sir,' he replied innocently, like one of my students. A shooting star slid across the sky as straight as a die, reminding me to the omniscience of the heavens. I looked up to the night sky to see millions of distant stars forming the bulk of our galaxy and I heard the distant sound of my father and later, the gentle beat of his belt on to my back.

Bring my mad mind back to Earth. Fix my sanity on to these streets.

There would be a thousand things to ask later that night. A young man who happened to be in the bar, that hour, that minute. Oh dear Lord, how much trouble comes from that which happened to be?

*   *   *

I returned to my sister's passing no one, the streets deserted, the world seemingly abandoned. The weather had turned bad or is there no such thing as bad weather, only wrong clothes. I would not wear these clothes again. My chest was pumped with pride, steps marching like the Queen's Guard. The key was still kept in the pot to the right of the front door, that sea blue monstrosity shipped from an Arab in a rip-off store in the heart of Marrakech. I turned the lock, left to right, and then quickly from right to left; a sojourn in time. I closed the door behind, the gentle noise reminding me of the early hammerings of a distant nail into an, as yet, unseen coffin. I slovenly tiptoed up the stairs remembering the seventh one up had a creak that would wake the entire house. Thank heaven I visited only once a year; the whole procedure to reach my room would definitely finish me off if it were repeated weekly, let alone daily. I fell onto the bed and closed my eyes, relieved that it was over, a long, long day. As I closed my eyes, I thought of saying a prayer, to pray for me and my faith in resurrection . . . but I did not.

*   *   *

I stood up. I felt suddenly dizzy. The room turned into quick circles and went white. Next thing I remembered was that I had had a dreamless sleep.

'Lunch Clifford!'

I cupped cold water in my hands and splashed it over my face . . . I glanced in the mirror. Oh dear God, dear God, what a state!

'Clifford, hurry up, food is ready!'

Sweet mother, I am coming. 'I will be down in five minutes,' I yelled. I slapped cologne on, sweet as lemon. I suddenly felt better, and to celebrate my fresh rejuvenated face, I snatched a bottle of gargle and washed my mouth with mint. A new man, fresh face, fresh breath and years younger. 'To recovery,' I mumbled, 'to peace and plenty!'

'The woods have been cordoned off. There was a murder late last night . . . in Wimbledon of all places.' My sister was relaying the day's news as I waited for my lunch to be served. The clock on the wall said it was past two o'clock.

'Did you see anything suspicious last night, Clifford?' she asked.

The damn question resuscitated my hangover, 'No,' I answered. This could well have been the worst hangover of my life but isn't that how all hangovers seem at the time. It was fast becoming clear to me that my drink might well have been tampered with the night before. I could usually take my doubles better than that. Perhaps the greasy foreigner slipped something in; it had happened before and would no doubt happen again.

I felt uneasy and began to eat my lunch in keeping with my heavy mood. I summoned courage and chewed an overdone steak with slightly burnt potatoes into my mouth. Very unappetising, but I had a slight sense of relief that my confused mind had not totally put me off the food.

'Some cheese, Clifford?'

I took one look at the gelatinous substance that closely resembled the regurgitation of a pigeon. 'No thank you, sister, I have to go out.'

I set off to the pub and slammed the door behind, the light decidedly grim. Different pub this time, something more speckled!

Aaarh that was better! A double-double. The barman gave a scowl but sod him too. The drink was helping with yet another recovery. This was definitely number one in top ten of all time great hangovers. The talk was about the local murder. I couldn't get in a word edgewise. Not that I cared, instead I retreated to the corner to read the evening paper. I looked at the front page, the black bold print headline leaping in front like a leprechaun. '*MURDER ON WIMBLEDON COMMON*'. I skimmed the story to the middle paragraph, which described a sighting of two young men walking arm in arm to the vicinity of where the victim was recovered, and I quote: '*The lacerated body was found by a local woman walking her dalmatian just before seven o'clock this morning, the body allegedly covered in blood under a makeshift bed of leaves*'. Poor, poor dog, it must have the most terrible shock.

'Excuse me,' a man from Calcutta yapped. 'That is my paper,' and snatched it back like the foreign beggar he is. And although his impertinence urged me to clear off, I stood to buy myself another round. As I made my way to the bar, I caught my reflection in the Double Diamond mirror. Someone had drawn black circles round my eyes like marking a calendar with important dates. I stood still, paused, and reflected that I live my life with fear of dying from boredom, perched on a bar stool staring ahead into my deep gloom. I missed D and the rest of the boys at that moment and realised that I had found my vocation, the education of the young.

'Drink up, we are closing' the Landlord called, as dull as a piano being tuned. I cursed the fact that I did not have time to order another.

As I left I noticed the early fall of snow, at first gentle but when I turned into our street, a deluge of flakes. They were my company as the street was deserted. My shoes drenched, my suede ruined. I coughed and coughed. Damn! I was coming down with a cold, my head throbbed and throbbed again. By the time I knocked on the door, I had a temperature. Straight to bed with a hangover and flu; the devil's mix. I felt like I had been shot, but could see no blood.

'Yes to bed you go,' ordered my sister and I heard my mother, my dear mother with her razor sharp teeth that could chop off a piece of flesh from animal or human and gobble it away without trace, without guilt like a butcher with his meat cleaver. Yes my dear mother, Blofeld's piranha, the mother of all piranhas.

I was sick for days – no drink, no fags. Yes, I was that sick! Just the occasional knock on the door to bring in the food, 'Stay away young Sean, it may be catching,' I moaned. Dear nine year-old Sean who wanted to get in my bed and cuddle up to make me feel better. The forced rest made me calm and perhaps I needed to simply be still for a while. The lights suddenly went out in my head and I slept with the ringing of a boy's choir singing 'to hell with you all' in perfect time, in perfect voice. I had a fever.

'You were calling for mother,' remarked Jean and I groaned. Jean's hair swept back not unlike mother's and her scent, lavender, yes the smell of lavender; mother's smell as she held me in her arms when I was so young, not past my sixth birthday; me the innocent, the helpless.

By Christmas Day I had been transformed back to full strength, clear head, no longer suffocated by trivial thoughts. Yes, quite the man again. Let's celebrate with a shot of my favourite refreshment. I offered myself the vague excuse, that not drinking for more than five days would create a tremendous shock to the body. If I was to 'give up the booze and the one night stands', to quote the man who wrote *Baker Street*, it would be gradual. My sister would, over the next day, throw the occasional glance, the scolding type when I helped myself to drink.

'You drink like father,' she would say and I would reply, 'He needed to. I do it spontaneously and for pleasure.'

Presents were bought before I left Norfolk. All wrapped in cheap local newsagent Christmas paper; a glossy Osmond calendar for young Sean, who politely said a thank-you but clearly was disappointed. Bath oil for my dear sister and a tie for her husband, a crazy mesh of colours, name one and it was there: Rhubarb reds and pewter greys, aubergines and cinnamon, electric blues and the whites of lilies; sapphire, silver, beige, orange, nougat, vermilion, opal, yellow, amber, green and ebony. 'Lovely Clifford, that is just what I needed.'

I, in return, received a blue and yellow scarf of my favourite football team, Shrewsbury Town! 'But, dear sister, I support Arsenal.'

'Do you?'

'Ever since I was five, dear sister. You must remember your little brother setting off with father to the underground with his RED AND WHITE scarf tied to his neck? Father's hand clasped to mine.'

'No I don't.'

'But you must! Little Clifford keeping his footsteps exactly on the cracks of the pavement and dear father, as if walking a tightrope between boredom and relaxation, loneliness and solitude, frustration and acceptance.'

I had my appetite back and I was not alone. For the day, Jean lost her fight with gluttony and gobbled down every remaining pea and chipolata on her plate.

'That's my girl,' cooed Donald, aroused by the greed. They are a small family, all munching away, many smiles, much laughter. Jean would be talking and in my eye occasionally freeze, stung by time, and again mother would return.

Donald brought in the Christmas pudding, on fire and crammed with sixpences.

'Not too much, Sean, it is laced with brandy,' his father advised.

'Clifford, would you like Christmas pudding?'

'Yes Donald, two extra slices please and I would also like to make a toast . . . To my dear sister and her wonderful family, a big thank you. You have made me learn to laugh again, which for starters can only help because when you laugh, you are usually not thinking of yourself.'

With our stomachs full, we moved in front of the television. 'Just think of it, the murderer is still on the loose and might be watching the Queen's speech just like we are now,' the tiresome Donald observed.

The speech was like an escalator breaking down mid-way through the climb. What is it about the masses that marvel at this piece of hypocritical crap? There she sits making me squirm as the country stops talking and stares at the black and white screen. I felt trapped like cattle shut in a pen, so close together that they shit in each other's eyes. Get me out of here!

'I will be leaving the day after tomorrow.'

'But Clifford, I thought you were staying until New Year and you spoke so kindly earlier.'

'Sorry, dear sister, I have been called back to school. They are working out new timetables and want, or probably need my help.'

Did I notice a muffled sigh? She was probably shocked that I did not start weeping. But don't despair dear sister, life goes on outside with its vindictive blend of screams and laughter. Don't be so sensitive. I think it is important to be insensitive to such emotions. Perhaps you haven't suffered enough; for me, all gentle tiptoes at night and the continual lectures of not being good enough, suffocated that emotional vein. I have suffered enough. I never had the school master putting his reassuring arm round my shoulder saying, 'I am terribly sorry,' or a priest looking into my eyes and offering a consoling word or a chance to confess. No I was left to face my demons alone dear sister with the persistent tut from our father.

73

I noticed my sister was reverting to type and taking on the role of mother without a hint of a strain. My mother, who kept still in her high-heeled slippers, floral dressing gown and curlers, witnessing what was happening in her middle class house in Wimbledon, on a suburban road, year in, year out. She gave no clue of what was happening other than having her nose held in the air as if there was a bad smell. She took her secret to her grave, to the Wimbledon mud. Our mother, who, after her stroke, died a few months later when she fell, just over there, at the foot of the stairs.

'Basically her brain collapsed,' the doctor rather too jovially announced.

I picked up the mood and said, 'Doesn't that happen often enough when we're alive!'

She was cremated under smoke-like fog, attended by her two children and select friends, all proud in their role of suffering together the sight of someone else's death. 'I am terribly sorry faces', recounting what a fine woman indeed Mother was.

'Clifford, are you all right?'

'Yes, dear sister.' I looked at the pen on the kitchen table and removed from my mind, as it were, the firm tick against 'forgiveness'. Better said, I crossed the top of the tick, in the manner I mark my students' work when I wish to convey that an answer is partly right, partly wrong.

*   *   *

The train pulled out of Liverpool Street Station and headed to the wet Norfolk coast. Oh to spend New Year on my own without family! I shuffled and stirred with fellow passengers, all likewise making their escape. A gentle whiff of being grateful consumed our carriage. I turned to the window and the winter gloom gave the countryside a sense of peacefulness.

74

My imagination got to work and I fantasised about the boys waiting for my return: 'No more holiday for me mummy, I want to get back and spend the last few days with Mr Coles.' I shuffled again in my seat as if I was about to recite some lines. But I would say few words in the coming days, instead be in company of my mantelpiece, bare of invitations.

A child sat nearby making far too much noise. Side glances from the little urchin, the type that rips off his teddy's head with a sharp knife he stole from his parents' kitchen. Can't you control your own fucking children? I would have received a wallop . . . a firm hand across my ear, the colour of a beetroot.

A nun passed as I walked to the school. I touched her with my eyes and believed she blushed. Avalanches of melting snow fell from the rooftop and released a thud. No other sound, no one to be seen, the only sound was the thawing snow. The headmaster and Mrs Draper were out of town, far away in deepest Exmoor surrounded by fellow ghouls; thank God for that. I decided to take charge. I was to be the headmaster for the week. Clifford Coles, headmaster of Falston; it had a ring to it.

I unpacked my case and immediately swaggered along the corridor to the headmaster's office. I thought it would be suitable to try my throne, the chair behind his desk, soon to be my chair behind my desk. But the bugger had locked his door. I turned and turned the handle but it was no use.

'Fuck it,' I fumed. I was defeated and very cold. The heating had been switched off and the corridors were as cold as an abattoir. 'Good afternoon,' I simply said out loud and headed to the headmaster's private quarters. This time the head had left his door wide open, so much so, I thought someone might be inside. 'Headmaster!' I called out. 'Headmaster, are you there?' The door creaked, needing oil. I thought I might buy some in town the following day and do some handy work.

'Go on in,' I heard the voice in my head plea. 'This will one day be all yours.' I went straight to the drinks tray. It was full of Christmas presents with fawning words written on seasonal cards hanging from the bottlenecks. 'Happy Christmas headmaster, best wishes, Major General Swindale, Chairman of the Governors.'

I almost puked and to make myself feel better, I opened his gift of a mediocre bottle of sherry. 'Fuck you!' I toasted and started to pace. Ironically, I usually enjoy such a 'pacing mood' because it is one of the few occasions on which I feel I get somewhere near the fringes of meditation. I eventually sat down drinking my third glass from the sofa, my eyes rolling around as if following flies. I was looking for something concealed, something out of the ordinary. I asked myself: are we likely to see things more clearly if we do not look too closely? But that triggered a list of questions such as: are things more likely to happen if we don't try too hard? So I decided to keep moving and snoop further into my future quarters.

Their bedroom was a colourless, foot odour-reeking room. Mrs Draper's crimson dressing gown had been laid out on the bed without a crease, as had the head's yellow pyjamas. Lying beside was a pair of hand knitted socks the colour of a peacock; no doubt finished by his beloved wife whilst he slept at the end of a tiring day in front of the fire; their lives rocking laboriously to the pulse of another ghastly Christmas. To the bathroom, and surprisingly, the shower had not quite been turned off. The running water was scalding and dashed the glass, looking like droplets of milk bouncing about in a bucket. I began to turn it off but stopped, paused and gently increased the pressure. I took off my clothes. I showered all over, shaved all over, dressed all over.

Quite refreshed, I decided to take my inspection of the school. It was not long before I reached the empty dormitories. The beds had been made, the sheets tightly tucked in by the holiday cleaners. I found D's bed, his tartan blanket no longer there, packed away in his trunk for the holidays. My head started to ache as if struck by a nail. I laid down on his pillow, my legs hanging over the edge. How like coffins these prep school beds are. I smelt the remnants of his scent against the pillow. I inhaled a deep breath and immediately felt content again. I closed my eyes and in the silence I could hear his breath, the sound when he was running on the rugby field, slightly short, a gentle despair.

By the bedside on a chair, there was a bible, a small pocket edition in blue leather, well thumbed. I picked it up and started to turn the pages. A photograph of D's mother fell to the floor. It was taken in colour, a Polaroid. The background was that of a racecourse, probably Ascot. She had a wide smile and a wide hat and was posing next to a horse playing the role of the contented owner. 'Look happy,' the photographer would have ordered and she had played the role to perfection. How truly beautiful she was, God's creation. I had found his mother's picture tucked away in his bible strangely moving. Perhaps I was turning into a sentimental fool? I let out a yelp. Perhaps I heard something and wanted to see if anyone was there. No! Just silence, a moment's silence to allow the angel to pass overhead . . . or beneath. I took down my trousers, smelt the freshness of my body, and thought it was better to masturbate in heaven rather than fuck in hell. The wank did not last long but it will be considered on my death bed as one of my best.

As soon as it was finished, I fell asleep for not more than half an hour. I slept lightly, always very near to waking. As I opened my eyes, for a moment I forgot where I was and then I looked at the rows of empty beds. I am home I thought, where I belong. I stood, wiped my sperm away with a rug from a neighbouring bed (poor little sod), picked up the bottle and empty glass. I held the bible again and took the picture out. This will be mine I thought and I tucked it into my inside pocket. Suddenly I was overwhelmed by hunger. I would go to the Greek to celebrate the New Year; fill my belly with wine and moussaka.

There was a fidgety silence in the restaurant. I sat at my usual table and immediately spilt my drink, knocking blood-red wine onto the white tablecloth, soaking it in like blotting paper. The Greek taverna's music disappeared into the rafters high above the moussaka. 'You are alone, Mr Coles?'

'No I am joined by my crowd of voices, so go away you nosey Greek sod and, before you go, pour some more wine and bring me my bloody food.' I was ravenous. I had anticipated the mediocre Greek cooking for days and when the food finally arrived, a youngish waiter flashed a forced smile and said, 'It is fine to have you back' or something tedious. I had not noticed our young Greek friend before.

'OK you can stop smiling now you little tart.' I recognised that lewd manner from a summer in Brazil where young whores with their copper bodies tarted like flies round a piece of fresh meat. The damn tease with whorish swagger and the wallet sucking grin. I was advised not to be misled by their cute smiles and wailing but I did not listen and the meat began to rot and the flies multiplied.

The roar of an engine parked outside disturbed the silence of the restaurant. In trooped a group of four – all noise, all swagger, potential fornication. The local playboys with their girls covered in pancake makeup and Ratner jewellery. Although the restaurant was empty, they sat on the neighbouring table. God do I hate that. Like going to an afternoon picture show and someone sits right next to you when they could have chosen a hundred other seats. They talked of money and laughed at their ignorance about anything, about everything; no education, no breeding. I was about to tell them to shhh, until one, the king amongst his unbeautiful flock, offered a drink.

'Yes and make it a double.' He smiled and made no fuss of my cheeky order. The charm of this prosperous working-class oik made me feel, let's say, generous in spirit. I caught a quick glimpse of one of his girls and flashed a lemon tasting grin. 'Have another,' he whispered so close that I felt the tip of his tongue deep in my ear. I kept my composure and accepted with grace. I thought, 'If only we could be alone,' perhaps he gets his sexual kicks out of making love to strangers in front of his best friend's wife. Randy sods!

'What do you do?' the king asked.

'I am a teacher.' He did not seem remotely interested.

'I make money,' he said.

'And you clearly like it.'

'What is there not to like?'

'Well everything has its drawbacks. You have to lock your front door for one, to keep the wolves and the taxmen away!' I continued, 'Money can't buy peace of mind and it can't buy time. 'Lay not up treasures on Earth, where moth and rust doth corrupt, and where thieves break through and steal, but lay up treasures in heaven, man, where doth must not corrupt . . . ' But someone who is broke at least doesn't have to make decisions, they can simply and always say 'No!'

'Let me get you another drink, teacher,' the king said. I sensed a hint of sarcasm. He was the sort that treated every-thing except money as unimportant. His girlfriend tugged on his arm with a hint of jealousy. He was paying far too much attention to me. She did not like it. This made me feel good. 'I have been trying to break up with her for months,' he whispered in to my ear. Of course you have, like a relationship that is forever ending, 'This is definitely "it",' but next fucking day, the fucking thing has fucking started again; like a novel that is forever 'nearly ready' but the deadline is constantly changing and moving further and further ahead.

Suddenly the room began to stir, the king's mouth moved in slow motion. I held on to my chair believing that the room was turning round in circles. And there was that throb again until, bang, I remembered no more until it was time to be ushered out of the restaurant. My head had apparently been lying on the table. One of the waiters shook me vigorously and when I came round, they were laughing and saying, 'Too much drink!'

'I beg your pardon; there is no need to be rude!'

Where were their manners? And to comment on my behaviour! I was beginning to think that they were decent sorts of human beings. I had no compunction to scold them, instead I asked where had the oiks gone?

'They left Mr Coles and paid for your dinner.' Well wonders will never cease, generosity and style on the coast of Norfolk. I walked home refreshed from my black-out, a miracle cure to behold. The coloured light bulbs and Christmas trees hung pathetically along the street, presumably for the benefit of the locals but it was past midnight and the only evidence of life was a rat that scampered across the wet street shy of noise, a lonesome rat on an ordinary day. It scurried away to spend the night on its own, not unlike me, with the instinct to hide when wounded.

I was so drunk that I opened my shirt collar to piss. I spelt my name out with urine: C–L–I–F–F–O–R–D C–O–L–E–S and then energetically pulled the chain and watched my work flush away, listening to the water flow down the elderly copper pipes into the bowels of the sewer. And for a moment I looked at the chain and imagined myself hanging by the neck until I swung, only to be discovered days later by a boy on his first day back at school; a new term, a new beginning. The thought made me relax. A sudden peace flowed through my body, the thought of death creeping in. But then without invitation, a shiver of pain, perhaps fear, jerked through my skin like an alarm in the middle of the night and I walked away back to my room and crashed fully clothed on top of my bed. It was well before the clock had struck to welcome in the New Year.

*   *   *

We were sharing an evening tipple and discussing my beliefs again on the need for social rules and fabric versus personal freedom, when the geography teacher quite suddenly said: 'You have not been looking your best recently Mr Coles.'

I thought he was simply trying to assert himself.

'You're fucking joking of course!' But when I noticed the geography teacher's tightening of mouth and general blanching of the face, I knew he was telling the truth. I was beginning to let myself go. We cut short our drinks and I hurried to the bathroom to gaze straight into the mirror with self-loathing eyes. My hair was rather limp, and I had the dishevelled appearance of someone who had dressed rather more quickly than he might have wished. I performed some emergency work to be more presentable. I straightened my tie and smoothed down my hair, like a schoolboy on his way to his first exam. That was better! In truth it had to get better! The future headmaster should always look presentable. My father for years marched with a swagger as if he was going to some important diplomatic meeting. 'Always look your best,' he would advise and, 'Believe in yourself because if you don't, no one else will!' It is frequently said that if you say anything frequently enough, you will end up believing it. For example, if you say anything frequently enough, you will end up believing it; if you say anything frequently enough, you will end up believing it; if you say anything frequently enough . . . 'I will be headmaster of Falston, I will be headmaster of Falston.' And then who should come to the rescue and offer an escape from the recent bout of insecurity but the headmaster. It was as if he had thrown a

81

blanket over my tired body. Is there anything quite as nice as having a blanket put over you when you are tired and inebriated?

'I have to go to Mrs Draper's sister's wedding,' he announced and generously offered a pair of football tickets for the coming Exeat weekend. How unexpected his gift was; like a sudden cold wind on a hot day or YELL in what was thought to be an abandoned house.

'Thank you, headmaster, I will take my nephew,' I lied. The last time I had gone to a football match was five years before and a photograph of me standing by the pitch was taken on that day. I had completely forgotten about it although the photograph had sat on my desk for some time. Wide open mouth, self-loving eyes caught in the right light, a time in my life with every angle gorgeous. Is it vain or commendable to have photos of yourself in your own room? I suppose it depends on your reasons for having them there. Is it for sweet memory's sake or purely for the kindling of the ego or for the inducing of resentment? And it also depends, of course, on whether you look good!

I did not want nor need company; I would take the opportunity of not only watching the match but also having a proper haircut and buying myself a new jacket.

The train to Arsenal was packed with men singing for their football team. Faces stacked together so close you could hear the different key of man's breath, fast breathing like randy bulls. They all had the confidence, indeed swagger, that their team would win and their chants matched the expectation. What a repugnant bunch they were, with bellies swinging in perfect unison to the jolts of the train, hands in their pockets, fondling their cocks to check their testosterone.

As soon as the train arrived at the station, the doors swung open and we were pushed on to the platform by a surge as remorseless as the sea. I weaved up the escalators avoiding the foul mouth singing and the onset of a skirmish.

The shadow of the stadium followed my steps. As I approached the main stand the vast over-hang made my unconscious feel uneasy. 'Come on,' I whispered, 'try to enjoy yourself.'

'Do you have a spare ticket, mister?' An adorable oik, sleek, effortless in his action, tight lips, whored his question in front of my eyes. He had a red and white scarf tied to his wrist ready to be held aloft in adoration for his team.

'How many are you looking for?' I asked, my left hand deep in my pocket fondling the headmaster's gift.

'Just for me,' he replied.

'Too bad, if I had one, it would be yours.'

I felt tempted to give him my extra ticket but my fingers had gone numb and my feet were beginning to lose grip. I needed time for myself.

His mouth drooped and suddenly his whole demeanour changed. His disappointment written on his face with a pained grimace, his shoulders slumped and he carried himself away as if he needed a good night's sleep. Before walking through the turnstiles, I grabbed my spare ticket and tore it into shreds; it flew to the sky like a sudden snow shower. I had felt tempted to give it away, but this was my time to be alone, alone with my thoughts. However pretty he may have been, it was not worth the risk of having temptation so close.

The stadium was packed for the visit of Manchester United, changed into white shirts so as not to clash with the home team. The crowd greeted the teams in a deluge of sound, thousands on tiptoes, two fingers in the air flung at the visiting supporters.

A whistle was blown and a surge of anticipation released; the previous hours' anxieties melted into the memory. This was a new beginning, another chance. I refused to fall in the way many other schoolteachers have followed; letting themselves go with the rigour of responsibility and plain old loneliness. I had always been regarded as a handsome fellow and although drink had begun to take its toll, I made a vow that the booze was not going to triumph; I clenched my fist and acclaimed my salvation. 'If only . . . if only,' was not going to be the last chapter of my life.

By half time, there were still no goals. The best action followed during the break. A group of Mancunian imbeciles had invaded the home team support. First they raided in dribs and drabs and then converged like a pack of wolves; the police moved in brandishing truncheons and shelling out fists. It was becoming quite the entertainment. I was transfixed, even excited, by the anger and frustration of the mob. What they needed was a good fuck. I heard my voice cry out loud. My neighbours gasped slightly. A slight gasp of fear resembling the moment at a funeral when due to the weight of the coffin, the body might be dropped from the pallbearer's shoulders. I had begun to prepare myself for a good old-fashioned killing when the teams emerged from the tunnel for the second half.

The opposition went ahead within minutes of the restart, and as forty thousand home worshippers began to pour scorn on their heroes, I stood up and decided to make my way out to the exit. 'Hey mate, where's your respect, we will support you evermore.' I had better things to do than to sit and hear the moans and groans of the fickle football supporter. I stepped onto the street and smelt the blood of the impending battles. I had enough. I was heading to the West End.

As I bought my tube ticket I heard a massive roar, an explosion of sound and of relief radiating from the home support. There is a God after all; the masses were praising the Lord. I left the area not looking over my shoulder but running towards a sane and sober afternoon and recognised that I had not once thought of the boys back at school; perhaps there was a life outside the school gates after all.

*   *   *

'Sir, may I recommend a short back and sides. Slightly long, if you don't mind me saying, and you should certainly have a manicure.' I looked down and saw dirt wedged into my nails. Yes, cleanse the dirt from the soul. At that moment I desired to be very clean, with the intensity only the innately dirty can comprehend. God is for sinners! For I now rendered myself pure in body, mind and soul. I remind myself that the present can be stopped at any moment and therefore a new future begin.

He plucked his chin as if musing on the appropriate first snip and started without giving me time to answer, a true professional, and a master at work. The haircut did not last long. He worked his craft quickly and within a short time I looked ten years younger. My oiled hair now parted to the side. Yes, I looked my best, my young self, hair glistening, eyes bright. A change so sudden that I half expected the salon to break out into instant applause, even cheer. I sat in silence wafting in the new me.

'May I suggest, sir, that you always ask for this style? You look quite . . . what is the word I'm looking for? That's it . . . handsome.' Was that a blush I detected on the barber's face, plus a twitching of the head and a more staccato shuffling of the feet? He splashed my face with some home-brewed cologne, brushed down my jacket, and said. 'Twenty pounds!'

'Shit,' I cried.

'I beg your pardon,' I heard him utter.

'Just the price,' I replied.

'Excuse me, sir, gentlemen never complain about that sort of thing.' He suddenly leant forward provocatively, almost as if he wanted to be strangled. I thought for a moment that he was going to give me an embarrassingly juicy kiss.

He smirked and I dug my fingers into his shoulder. I could feel my varnished fingernails dig deep into his flesh.

'OK, OK, pay me fifteen,' he finally conceded.

So I relented, letting go of his shoulder and paid the scoundrel with no tip. As I headed to the door I said under my breath, but loud enough for him and the waiting few to overhear, 'Would you like me to tell your wife that you like your arse to be tickled by a duster.'

I reneged on the promise to buy myself a new jacket and instead caught a bus to Liverpool Street and headed back to Norfolk. As I sat on the top deck and saw the reflection of a fine hair cut in the window, I mused that my reaction earlier had been most unfair. A belief in the eventual power of good should not entail the blind denial of bad. If I wanted to get better, I had to at least acknowledge that.

*   *   *

It was the annual visit to the funfair on the sea front. The posh boy's amalgamation with the hoi polloi in bumper cars and 'Kiss me Kate' hats. The weather suited my mood, damp and grey; typical British seaside weather. Mr Lloyd, dull Mr Lloyd, my second in command with the care of twenty-five boys each with a spring in their step and flushed faces, their conversation hurried like a gramophone record going full speed. Liberation for us all amongst the dodgems.

'Can I go on the big wheel, sir?' D asked, life folding up in front of his eyes.

'Of course you may.' D reminded me every day that he is a cut above everyone else. Even the way he asked that simple question was with charm and beauty. His beautiful brown eyes and mock mournful gaze.

'Let me give you this,' I handed him a freshly minted six pence piece from my pocket and placed it into his hand.

He gave me a wave as his seat reached the summit. 'Look at me, sir!' I caught my breath and needed to sit down. The monster of the wheel spun round. 'Look at me, sir.' His voice dominated my mind, dominated the noise of the rides, the murmur of conversation, the half-laughs, the blaring music from broken speakers. 'Look at me, sir.'

'Can we go on the dodgems, sir, please sir?' Proudlock asked. D was standing alongside, pulsating from his ride on the big wheel.

'Be careful,' snatching at my tone like tearing open a letter.

And off went the boys scrambling to find a suitable car. D held his hand up at one of the yobbos like a priest blessing a congregation. He handed the inked, thick Neanderthal the fare. Blessed are the pure in heart . . . and without a mere 'thank you' from the working class oik, D drove away immediately bumping into another car. The beauty on his face, the howl of laughter; why can't we be so happy all the time?

I pray to Jesus Christ that life will turn out fine, onto my weak knees to the son of God. Away from the sight of the boys I arched like a man you expected to see when weeping, crippled with sorrow. Dear God, why is it when happiness greets us, that we turn to the Almighty for reassurance? I needed a drink, a bottle of wine. One of those bottles at the local liquor store lined on the top shelf, so orderly it resembles a choir in red cassocks.

'Can I win a goldfish, sir, and give it to you?' asked Proudlock.

'No you bloody can't! And don't tart boy!'

'But please, sir?'

'Yes please, sir?' joined D.

'Of course you can, my boy, I would be honoured.'

Mr Lloyd tutted rather too loudly, clearly noticing my favouritism. And off they went and, would you believe it, won the sodding goldfish with the first throw of a ping-pong ball.

'Here you are, sir,' D handed it over and purred like a sentimental cat.

'Thank you,' I said, faking a smile. 'I shall call it David

after King David.' But now I have to find a fucking bowl to put it in.

*   *   *

I felt I had become a little tetchy with Proudlock of late. He is a sad little boy. He came in search of me at the beginning of term. Knock on the door just before the boys' bedtime. I thought I had heard his gentle breathing outside in the corridor for quite some time before he plucked enough courage to disturb my free hour before prep. I did say after all that I was always here to help.

After the third knock, I called out 'Yes!' This fragile figure wearing blue pyjamas and a grey dressing gown tiptoed in.

'Just to talk about my work, sir.' Come on in boy. I instinctively knew that he had more to say than just being concerned with his B in the History paper of last term. Let's just call it a teacher's hunch, teacher's intuition. I poured him a glass of water.

'I also find it difficult to admit what's really on my mind.' I soothed, 'I can see something is bothering you. It will be our secret, I promise.' To my amazement, he laid out his problems in front of me like a pack of playing cards. The list was long from the basic homesickness, 'I miss riding my horse' to the headline stealer of his father regularly hitting mother 'right in the nose.' I was genuinely moved as his face creased with pain. I wanted to sing him a soft lullaby, 'We're here because we're here because we're here,' but refrained and instead sank deeper into my chair and let him purge his darkest secrets. I am a good listener given the chance. The grimace as he spoke of his father's temper moved me to near tears. I felt it in my bones that he had beaten the boy into pulp. I wanted him to admit it.

'Tell me, boy,' I urged, but he spoke only of his mother's beatings. I felt it was my duty to know and for an instant considered it my duty to take action. I swore the next time I saw Proudlock Senior, that I would walk straight up and tell him if he ever laid a hand on his son again, I would report him to the authorities. Proudlock Senior, with his grey and forlorn face, who I judged on our first meeting to be the sort of person who would be on anyone's side as long as the anyone thinks on the same line as he does. Now I think of it I am sure his wife muttered to me once, 'The easiest man to get along with if he gets his way.' The type who loves babies if they don't cry or wet nappies, dogs if they don't bark, foul the carpet, or stare at him and wives if they produce.

As he spoke, tiredness caught up and I saw Proudlock yawn as wide as a hippopotamus.

'Sorry sir.'

'No need to be sorry, Proudlock. Better get to bed. You're not alone in this world, you have a friend here.'

The boy bowed his head and walked out without further word. I remained quite still, left with a medley of emotions: I was angry, surprised, concerned. I was in quandary what to do. I poured a drink and another, followed by a third. Do I need to get involved, turn the focus onto me? I was never the type that would come to the rescue if I witnessed an innocent being attacked on the street. I may tut rather too loudly but that was about all. By the time I had drunk a bottle of white wine, I'd made a decision. I'd say fucking nothing. That's what I'll say. Nothing! What a relief. But, of course, the relief did not last and voices in my head have become louder. Fuck off, guilty voice; you have not been invited to snigger. Perhaps that's why, whenever I hear young Proudlock's voice, I jump as if I am in a snake pit.

*   *   *

I retched and re-retched over the basin. That wasn't blood was it? Why don't I have my own garden so at least my dawn

89

chorus can scatter into the morning air? My first thought was 'Don't overdo it now.' It was the school's open day, a cavalcade of parents descending to see how Rupert or Harry was doing. Why don't they leave us alone? Leave for twelve weeks to guide their children? The fucking interference of it all. It is so easy to be nice to parents the first time you meet, less easy the second, and so on and so on; today I will be truly tested. The delicate time comes when you have to discard the platitudes, say politely 'piss off', though if I want to remain in this role I will be unable to do that. Oh to yell, 'Piss off!' and discard these interfering pricks. I want to throw parents like old bottles into a skip; a cemetery of spent bottles.

I glanced at my watch. Shit! I was running late. Today of all days the headmaster had organised a 'short' meeting in the common room, more like a speech – today of all bloody days. Luckily I had laid out my new summer suit on the chair, bought in a second-hand store on a street behind the Greek.

'Fits like a glove,' the Chinaman drooled as I tried it on. And he may have been right, the little Chink, greasing up for a potential sale. 'Almost new,' he said, probably because the previous owner would vomit on it repeatedly, seeing its colour. It is the colour of a pumpkin, no more, no less.

'Taken and bought, my good Chinaman.'

'That will be just two pounds!' he smiled to himself, satisfied. 'Finally got rid of that!'

The headmaster scolded us, for we seemed 'incapable' of getting into our classrooms on time. And many of us saw ourselves as University dons with the attitude that we were here to teach and stimulate but not too concerned with such matters as school rules. 'We are a prep school gentlemen, let's not forget that please.' Complete tosh of course, but there was an uncomfortable shift in the room whilst he was talking. 'Let's

impress the parents today with our overall attention to care.'
YES HEADMASTER.

The common room had been cleaned. We can't have a stray
parent walking in by mistake to witness the chaos of books and
overflowing ashtrays? Now can we? We were on show as much
as the boys. Best behaviour: 'How do you do, sir?' followed by
some fatuous remark like, 'You have to crack some eggs to
make an omelette!' The parents like that sort of repartee.

The roar of a hundred cars drove on to the school fields,
parked orderly round the cricket boundary. Mainly the blue
Volvo and the yapping dog stinking the car out. It was all
unpacked picnics, bottles of champagne and inane chatter. I
was umpiring the 1st XI (a fifteen over match). The geography
master was umpiring the colts. My choice, and he took it as a
huge compliment, which it was not.

The cricket field, the bastion of the English prep and public
school! As I stood behind the wicket, I felt mellow, a recon-
ciliation of all my internal quarrels. It was a scorcher of a day
and the sun egged onto my face. Perhaps that is my cure, the
Inca sun god roasting my body and the chaste smell of the
green wicket and oiled bat. The First XI won in fine style and
in record time, and being English gentlemen, the victory was
received in muted celebration. Robertson, the 1st XI captain,
approached after the match, pausing as if he was about to
hand out an award, and then thanked me for all my help in
sport and history – he is off to Eton. He carries the broad
lecherous smile across his face of someone that, in his future,
will win prizes galore. So good luck to him, and good luck to all
other buggers heading off to the Radleys, Harrows and Etons
of the world. I will miss none of you.

I was looking for D's parents. I had seen Mister earlier in
the afternoon and he had invited me to join them for some
'wine' after the game. I ignored the invitations from other

parents to join them to chat about their little Gregory or Robert or James . . . 'Must be going, thank you for the offer, such a pity . . . ' Some mothers fluttered their eyelids, like tails of angelfish, others gave themselves away with the flash of their lipstick smudged teeth. 'I must be going . . . ' The grey cashmere rug with D's parents sitting, drinking and eating turned out to be my sanctuary. I greeted 'father' like a boxer shaking hands. He made again an introduction to his wife Constance; she was friendlier than in recent times. D, majestic as always, seemed a little distant, probably due to the fact that he had dropped a catch in front of his parents. 'Don't worry about that,' I declared when the incident was brought up. 'It is never easy to catch on the boundary. From what I hear you were brilliant to even get near it.'

Constance suddenly asked D to walk with her. As they walked away, I heard the imaginary sound of a door being unlocked, bolt by bolt. She moved with her son's hand clasped to hers. I focused my eyes on the two figures striding across the cricket field, seemingly in a hurry to get away. The sun was right up and started to cast a shadow from where we were standing across their path in the direction of the green pavilion. I was offered more white wine, probably the best on the field.

'Yes, sir, or is it John?' Fill it to the brim, to the brim I say. We talked about cricket and we talked about his MCC membership.

'Took fifteen years to reach to the top of the list. Fifteen years – but the wait was worth it, sitting in the pavilion watching the greats pass through the Long Room to go out and bat. Would you be my guest this summer? England plays India in the next few weeks.'

'Yes John,' I quickly replied before he could change his mind. A summer holiday chance to spend more time with D. Is he a cricket whore, that young D? Will he indulge in cricket perversions with a cricket bat or with those vile prickly cricket gloves? Disgrace to have these thoughts but no one is telling are they . . . ?

Their departure was quite sudden. Constance returned, stretching her smile as she folded the rug and packed it neatly into the back of the car. If anyone needed a servant, it was at that moment. She turned only to remove another glass and pack it into the picnic basket, but the image I have as I write, is a woman with a veil pulled over, lips moving indefinably; she was eager not to meet anyone's eyes. Even when she asked me to look after her son in the coming weeks, her face was half hidden by shade, as if shadowed by a confessional grill. But what is her confession? Holy Mother of God, what will her first act of vengeance be, or am I mistaking her demeanour for her beautiful son's? Ah, the mystification of it all.

SUMMER HOLIDAY

I had left for London, free of a hangover. I had not had a drink for seven days! 'My name is Coles, I am an alcoholic . . . ' I had gone on what is known as a detox – a damn Americanism. I had glanced in the local bookshop at this 'Get Well in Five Weeks' book and was strangely seduced by its promises. I had even started to become the sort of person that washed his hands before meals. Soon I would be saying grace on my own and thanking the Lord for providing such a good life.

I had dressed in the pumpkin suit. They had seen it before on Open Day but I did not care, for it looked glorious on me. So there Mr Chinaman, Mr Chinkeroo, you with your slit eyes who thought only of his pocket, licking his thin lips when he sold it. It was a perfect summer's day. The early morning breeze blew through the open train window; no need for air-conditioning. Sitting opposite was a very good-looking creature pretending to read with a mournful expression on his face, 'Fear and Loathing in Las Vegas' by that buffoon Hunter S. Thompson – ostentatious crap. But his looks made me forgive his pretention.

'Good book?' I asked. He smiled back like a biblical creature with a fragrance of orchids. I tried to be cheery with the occasional cheery comment but he did not react, except once in a while to flash the whore's smile; all white teeth and full lipped. He was how I imagined my son to have been or perhaps to be like. Of course I don't mean this to be an incestuous aside. Far from it, Lord have Mercy, I am not my father for pity's sake! I have plans you see. It might be in a sea of deep paranoia or simply in the spotlight of suspicion, but I think the eyes of our staff room are pointed in my direction. I believe, or rather think, that their imagination is running away with them. They think I am perhaps a pederast! Shame on them! Mr Hankinson, who has never particularly taken to me, stopped gossiping as I barged into the staff room after a spot of history with 2A. I was sure that I heard my name and that of D's. I may not have thought anything more about it but the chill that wrapped round my body on that stifling hot day was, can we say, severe. Hankinson's jaw throbbed and 'Bible Basher' Chaplain Rev. Lowndes turned his back. He was no longer a fan of mine. After dinner, a few weeks before, he had tried to thrust his bible down my throat, pontificating about redemption and I said, 'Stick it up your ass!' He snarled by quoting Levictus: 'If a man also lie with mankind as he lieth with a woman, both of them have committed an abomination, they shall surely be put to death, their blood shall be upon them.' Hah . . . come the revolution he would hang me upside down with wire tied to my balls and a poker up my arse.

I plan to lay countless women in the coming months as a sort of charade. My father said that a man should behave this way, a public demonstration of inner deprivation, a show of superior masculinity. I will pinch matron's ass, attract the girls in town with my wicked and seductive tongue and, as a final laugh to my waiting public, I will be married in the local church in the eyes of God. Perhaps I will ask Rev. Lowndes to conduct the service and ask fellow masters and close relations to the knees-up. What a laugh, or should I say joke, that will be. This should lie to rest their search for anything untoward. This should hinder their cheap gossip. To the bride and groom they shall toast, 'May they be blessed with many children.' Cheers to that and the ordinariness that will prevail. 'Growing up is to settle for the cheapest version you can stand living with.' Whose quote is that, or is it one of mine?

There were three queues outside the Grace Gates at Lords. They shuffled uneasily, as if they were all dying for a piss. Well spoken, the air was filled with polite conversation. I was no different, 'Beautiful day for it John . . . thank you for the invite . . . those Indians know how to spin under these sort of conditions . . . ' Blah blah blah . . . John answered, making the most economical use of his time, whilst fishing out the day's tickets from the pocket of his perfectly cut trousers. D acted shy, not even a welcome handshake nor a 'Good-morning, sir'. Poor chap did not know how to behave. When you meet a master in the holidays, it takes time to realise that they have a life outside the school grounds; very understandable, and I recognised his reticence.

We sat in the Q stand; Q for queer I presumed. The morning session was dull. England batted and the Indians bored with their monotonous spin. D would ask his father the occasional question. His high voice pierced the summer's air. He sat the other side to his father. How I wanted to sit in the middle. I had imagined the previous night talking to John about fine wines and, more importantly, guiding D through the day's play. A woman, sitting right behind, sneezed particles all over the back of my neck. I turned round in fury but controlled myself as John was watching. I waited until we stood up for lunch and then whispered into her ear whilst no one was looking, 'You fucking plague-spreading bitch.'

As we walked towards the restaurant D pointed to where we were heading. 'This way Mr Coles, and mind yourself.' I thought he tried to grab my hand; the bliss of it all. I very nearly started to cry at the pure innocence of the moment. I wanted to pat his head as a thank you. I had to grab hold of my own hand to stop myself. I felt a shiver of guilt just thinking the dark thoughts that shot through my mind. I kept silently repeating to myself, 'Breathe through your mouth, Mr Coles. Breathe, breathe . . . '

John had booked a table in the dining room close to the stand, a collection of white-clothed tables served by charmless waitresses, eyes moving without faces. The military band, directly below from where we were sitting, struck up and bum note followed bum note. 'Bloody hell, what was that noise?' I said. John nodded, agreeing with my agitation. Taste I thought, you have to respect it. Although it was a minor thing, John's immediate recognition that we were listening to something turgid made our connection even deeper.

Just before I started to eat my watery pea and ham soup, a naval officer-type marched over with what looked like a small book of raffle tickets in his hand. Spick and span in a navy suit, tightly knotted minor public school tie, he roared, 'Money please . . . for three? That will be . . . ' He was collecting the cash for lunch. A damn right rip-off and bloody expensive. I put my hand into my empty pocket, pretending that I wanted to pay. 'Absolutely not, Mr Coles.' John took out a wad of perfectly ironed notes and carefully counted out the amount on the table. The naval man, in one action, pushed the cash into his fat pocket and without warning pinched D on the cheek. The sort of pinch your favourite perverted Uncle gives you when no one is looking. I could immediately tell that he preferred sodomy to any kind of work; the scoundrel. Neither John nor D looked surprised by his action but I refused to let it go. He walked away and I made an excuse that I needed to go to the loo.

'Of course,' said John, so I got up and walked to the bathroom but not before I passed my 'naval' friend. I leant over and spat words in his face.

'There is a section of the human race that is scum and should be crucified and buried alive in a deep grave or crucified on trees for the world to see their withered bodies. You will find that you have far fewer friends than you can imagine when you die.' The shock of eyes met his moustache. He mumbled and guffawed. His cheeks turned so red that they started to turn a deathly black. Ha, that will show him!

A plate of over-ripe strawberries was waiting when I returned. I poured the cream over and started to eat, one by one. The conversation was still and the silence was only broken by John asking, 'Coffee, Mr Coles?' I accepted, and we started to discuss the morning's play. Again D remained quiet but, to be honest, there was very little to add. There had been a total of eighty runs scored and not even a wicket.

'Let's hope the cricket is better this afternoon,' I said in stage whisper.

'It is still lovely to be here though.' John said, 'That is what I love about Lords, even if the game is not to your liking, the atmosphere makes up for it tenfold.'

'Of course, of course,' I greased a reply, hoping that I had not been over critical. As I walked out I noticed the naval type cowering in the corner. 'Have a good day,' I mouthed. He turned his head shamefully.

When we returned to our seats, God must have been watching for I found myself sitting between father and son. 'Sit down!' complained the old bitch sitting behind.

'Shall we swap?' I asked John.

'No, let's leave it for now,' he replied.

D finally relaxed and asked about the field positions of the Indian team. His questions were very astute. His voice dominated the murmur of all other conversations spreading across the ground. A mighty hit for six high into the pavilion. D stood and cheered, and for a second, an instant, he grabbed my forearm in excitement. FINALLY the touch of skin. 'What a shot!' I said, perhaps a little too enthusiastically. I saw my hand ruffle his hair and put my arm around his shoulders. God damn it Coles! I had started to laugh uncontrollably at the force of the action. Control yourself you fool. Have a glass of whiskey and five aspirins immediately. I made an excuse and set off to the bar.

'A very large double.'

The barman eyed me suspiciously. 'Another,' I ordered.

By the time I had returned to my seat, my eyes began to droop and drops of perspiration fell from my forehead. Shit, what an embarrassment. 'Are you all right?' asked John.

'Must have been something I ate,' I said, losing my breath.

'Poor Mr Coles,' soothed D. 'Is there anything I can get you?' I heard his words and when, only seconds before, life was seeping from my body, I suddenly opened my eyes wide and immediately felt better. It was as if he had given some emergency oxygen. I had risen from the depths of a hospital bed to a crescendo of lightness. All in a matter of seconds, because of a few syllables. The miracle of life!

By tea, I had regained my faculties. The feeling I might be sick at any moment had truly disappeared. Instead of sitting down for sandwiches, John suggested that we walk round the ground.

'Somewhat of a tradition and good for the constitution!' he said and patted his flat stomach. We set off and joined the queue of ten thousand who had also made the same decision. 'I hear that if you walk counter-clockwise round the ground it is slightly quicker, but I prefer this way,' announced John, ten minutes into a inch-by-inch shuffle so that half conversations became criss-cross.

I smiled spuriously and twitched in agreement. By the time we had reached where we had started, the first ball of the final session had been bowled. Thankfully, John said that we still had time to have a cup of tea. Being as distracted as I had been all day, I had completely forgotten about the flask tucked into the inside of my jacket; a hidden pocket near to its tail. I had never seen such an imaginative pocket in my life, made exclusively for my breed, the type that needs a surreptitious tipple. Thank you, Mr Chinaman.

D poured milk into my tea whilst he was distracted, talking to his father about their forthcoming holiday to France. I discreetly splashed a dram of whiskey into my cup. I had noticed my hand had begun to shake so much when I had tried to put my sandwich in my mouth.

'Daddy, can we go out on the boat as soon as we arrive?'

'I am sure we can,' John replied dismissively.

'Are you going abroad ,Mr Coles?'

Am I going abroad? I saw his mouth move and heard the words fall seconds later. This does not usually happen, but for a second I was lost. I had heard them talk about their holiday and I knew they had a villa in the South of France. Instinctively I answered, 'Yes, I always go to the Cote D'Azur.'

'That's where we go,' D exclaimed. 'We have a house there and . . . '

'Listen, Coles,' John said, 'we are minutes outside Cannes. If you are in the area, please call, come for the day, have a spot of lunch and don't forget your swimming trunks. Here's our number.' He scribbled it down in pencil on the day's menu.

'How lovely,' I replied, tore off the corner and folded the cheapish cardboard into my inside pocket. 'Yes, lovely,' I repeated quietly to myself.

I was so excited that the rest of the day paled in significance. Such a relief that I had something to look forward to; those long summer holidays can wear you out. There may have been some more wickets. In truth I don't remember, all I could think of was my future, the next two weeks.

*   *   *

I like the French, the shrug of shoulders, the muttering under the breath, the general pissed off snort; they remind me of me. How I wanted to leave these shores to spend time with them.

Heathrow was crowded with cretins. Lord help me. I lined myself behind a hideous family, all in matching tracksuits the colour of crimson. I held my breath, as if I were to catch something. I recoiled as if surrounded by snakes. Once, visiting India, my father advised, 'Be careful of snakes; if bitten by one, catch it, cut off its head and take it to the nearest hospital.' I never understood what he meant other than don't trust the buggers. He also warned never trust anyone who drowns his or her whiskey with an excess of water.

Children crossed from one side of the line to the other, each bumping into my legs. Not one of them gave me as much as a sorry. Dear God, where are these people educated? Their noise and their happy faces made me want to wrench.

'The flight to Nice is delayed for one hour, you have as requested, a window seat.'

'Thank you,' I answered, snatching my boarding pass away from the hand of the booking clerk. She seemed remarkably small crouched down on a stool, eyes directly looking over my shoulder at the repulsive family that I had overtaken when their youngest had fallen and cracked a front tooth. A delightful piece of luck, as I knew they would have taken an eternity to check in. I am in Hell, looking at God's imperfect creatures; Hell is everywhere, everywhere else.

To waste an extra hour, I went to WH Smith and browsed the magazine rack. A boy slouched by and I smelt his cheap branded scent. He hawked loudly and looked forward with a sick half grin on his face, satisfied with himself. Bored, he yawned, stooped to pick up a Crunchie and then picked up another and another. By the time he had finished, he had pocketed at least six. He swept them into his leather jacket, flicked his hair back and moved away to the exit. I loathed his slovenly attitude; he was a damn thief and for a second I thought that I should follow and scold him for his behaviour, give him some full-blooded Coles advice. But then he sealed his fate. He clearly knew I was watching, for as he was about to leave the store, he turned and repeated his whorish grin, but this time staring straight into my eyes. Enough, I decided, and marched up to the till.

'That boy has just stolen from your store,' I announced, pointing at the culprit. 'That boy in the leather jacket.' My hand was shaking with a mix of excitement and fury. The peasant of a woman looked up and focused her eyes on the thief.

'Do you mean him?' she asked, almost apologetically.

'Yes . . . him.'

'He's no thief, sir, he is my son,' interrupted a man not looking unlike an undertaker, 'and I have just purchased the chocolate.'

I thought for a second that he was about to ask for a duel; he had that sickly middle class tone.

'What, six bars?' I answered pathetically, knowing the blighter was flirting rather thieving.

'I am sorry for the misunderstanding, he does seem to carry a permanent look of mischief.'

*   *   *

I had it planned. I would spend two days on the beaches of Cannes, walk the Croisette like the movie stars during the festival, and when I have some colour on my face I will call D and invite myself to their glorious villa. Don't want to look too pale or indeed too desperate.

I'd booked into a *pension* that I saw mentioned in one of the Sunday broadsheets. 'A hidden gem,' the journalist had advertised. Probably getting a backhander from its owner. It was just behind the old port. A queen stood behind the desk asking me to sign this and to sign that. His hand was on his hip, left side slightly cocked. He spoke in French and I answered in English; the presumption of the man. He teased me with his face, and as he showed me to my room he raised his hand, looking like he was about to pull me towards him but instead, he only scratched his ear.

The room was small with a mock Persian rug covering the wooden floor. The bed was not unlike the one the boys slept on back at school; it was compact, wooden, and uncomfortable. A long window looked out onto hills and below I saw a hotel boy beating a blue and green carpet, the colour of a Californian swimming pool. When I awoke that morning I felt like death but the feeling had evaporated and now I felt remarkably fresh. I was born to live under the sun. Instead, I ended up living near bloody Norwich.

It was still early afternoon, so I decided to go for a stroll. I left my key with the queen and walked out into the warm air. A gaggle of boys loitered from the other side of the street. They stood in a group as if waiting for a victim. Not me, thank you very much. They looked like slum urchins for God's sake.

No sooner had I walked onto the front than a portly man swathed with cameras and souvenirs approached. 'Good price, good price!' He said, salivating with anticipation.

'JESUS,' I replied, 'I thought we were in the South of France, not fucking Morocco!' That told him and he shirked away, arms in the air shouting some Arab swear word.

'Algerians,' a passer-by whispered rather too loudly. I nodded my head in recognition of a kindred spirit.

I sat on the veranda of the Carlton Bar and looked out to the sea, calm and peaceful. There is nothing better than relaxing with a long drink under the sun, the afternoon heat warming your chest and neck. I was oblivious to those sitting near and was only distracted by a fly whirring round in wheels on the veranda floor. I considered whether I should stamp on it to free the insect from its misery. But instead I smiled as the fly died alone. I am sure I heard it scream. I sat out until the last remnants of the day's sun caught my face and gently burnt the skin. The veranda began to submerge in brown and yellow patches, an alcoholic brain seen close.

'Another drink, sir?' I saw the barman pour a whiskey from a special malt. I swallowed and as it fell to my stomach I felt a sense of finality.

'L'addition,' I called, snapping my fingers. I over-indulged with the tip. He was the perfect *garçon*, subservient and efficient. I virtually skipped my way back to the hotel. I had not felt so happy for months, or was it years? I made a note that when I retired from the rigours of headmastership, I would retire down here: a villa standing out from all else in the overpopulated hills, with the sunlight leaping across the land and at night, a strange living murmur of neighbours enjoying their late dinner under scattered stars which seem to be in perfect symmetry.

The restaurants were full, packed with frogs making a deluge of noise. One fell into the other, tables spilling onto the port side. Au Mal Assis had the most enormous tree, virtually splitting the tables in half. I found its sight disconcerting as I had dreamt of being stranded in a huge tree only the night before. I awoke feeling that the dream had consumed every second of my sleep; it had no reins, no boundaries. It had a sense of submission with fear submerging my very being like a claustrophobic morgue.

A waiter, seeing me standing in front of his restaurant, asked in English whether I wanted a table. He spoke with a tone, as if he had something up his sleeve.

'Yes, table for one.'

He smiled unctuously and led me to a table that stood directly behind the tree. He did not ask, he simply poured a glass of red wine and I drank the blood of France. How civilised.

As he poured I imagined what was beneath his white shirt. I grunted in code as I sipped from my glass.

He smiled in understanding and for an instant I intuitively knew that he was the type that dolled up in women's clothing during his off hours. I had read about various attacks on transvestites in the local Norwich rag. One was chased and caught by a gang near an amusement park and set upon. The chap was close to death before the police moved in to save the poor soul. Rumour has it that the police were watching until the very last moment. 'Should have let the gang finish him off,' remarked the geography master in a soft voice, while reading the article, slouching in his chair in the staff room.

'Ummm . . . '

'Really!' his voice rising so that the staff could hear his diatribe. 'Homosexuality is bad enough, but a deviancy of it is simply barbaric.'

I wanted to say, 'Better watch your step, "Mr Geography".' Instead I fell into one of my chilly silences.

I was at my most comfortable, revelling like an animal in new-found territory. 'May I have a menu?' I asked myself out loud.

'I am menu!' The waiter curiously replied.

My dinner followed: an assortment of seafood, other aphrodisia, the soufflé and a bottle of Armagnac, a grand reserve, simple and light. I drank the wine at a slower pace and listened to a full orchestra of language darting from one side of the restaurant to the other, merging into a gallimaufry. Still on their main course, some ogled their menus in an attempt to choose what to have for pudding; the food was that good.

The waiter was beginning to set my heart on edge. The randy little sod flirted shamefully, but I did my best to ignore his stares. I whispered in French when the Armagnac started to seep into my veins. I readily admit I was mighty drunk, but not too drunk to remember the name of my hotel to whisper it in my waiter's ear. I watched his face light up and give a smile of self-indulgence. It was as if he had been sent to the face of the earth to satisfy us all with animal anonymity; nothing degrading in that, unless one let himself be humiliated.

An old man shuffled from table to table, seat to seat asking for money, without much luck. And just as he left, up came a small boy, toes through espadrilles, cut off trousers and a torn dirty blue shirt. Give the poor boy some francs, look at his green, green eyes. Who says beggars should be abolished? I do, but for tonight I would make an exception. 'Here young man, take this,' and I handed him a note. An old woman glowered and wagged her finger 'He lies to you monsieur.'

'True, my dear, but tonight I do not care.'

It was early in a European sense when I called for my bill. The restaurant had remained busy and there were still a few asking for tables. It was then that I heard a familiar sound of laughter that coincided with the crashing of a bottle of wine. It was like a gun going off. In front, well two tables ahead and a large tree cutting the line of view, were D with mother and father. Dear God, how long had they been there? At that moment all I wanted was to piss. I could even hear John pronounce his vowels with suspicious care whilst Constance listened, aware that many eyes were set on her beautiful face. Decisions had to be made. Should I go and say hello or would the chance meeting seem suspicious? Why should that be, the encounter was genuine? Did the panic mean I was too drunk and therefore lacked the moral courage to introduce myself? Had I lost my touch of golden charm? God, I needed to piss. The bill arrived and I slapped down the exact amount. I had no time to respond to the fawning waiter. The buttons of his shirt lowered by two since the time of my arrival, showing a lithe hairless torso; the despicable tart. You know the name of my hotel, now piss off and I will see you later?

'Coles?'

'Hello there, what a surprise!' I replied, looking not at all surprised.

I was trying to reach the bathroom first before deciding whether to go over.

'Come and join us. Are you alone?' John insisted.

'No, my friend's just left.'

'Well, sit down then and join us.'

John immediately called over a different waiter and ordered another Armagnac. Constance put an arm over D's shoulders. John, slightly sloshed, talked about the fine weather. D said little, his brown skin breathing beneath a white summer shirt, the muscle on the top of his jaw throbbing. Pass me another drink. I left to go to the bathroom. Whispers followed my steps. My obsequious waiter jumped out at me just as I was about to undo my flies. 'No, not now, later . . . ' I shooed him away; how dare he presume. Returning to the table, I had sobered enough to realise that I should make my excuses and get the fuck out of there; I was beginning to babble and even I knew that was not a good sign.

'Forgive me, I have to get back to the hotel,' I said apologetically.

'I hope you will visit us tomorrow. Here is the address,' John passed a scrap of paper into my hand.

'Thank you,' and I was about to prattle on about this and that when a local came up to introduce himself to the table. I quietly backed away and left them to it, but not before D sank his eyes into mine pushing me into that twilight world between insanity and sleep.

*   *   *

An Englishman was complaining too loudly that there was no running water for his bath. 'But, monsieur,' the man at the desk said, 'the bath does not work, better to have a shower.' He started a game of charades putting his hands above his head and sprinkled with his fingers.

'But I don't want a shower, I want a bath.'

'Taps don't work, monsieur, for bath . . . use shower.' All of which resulted in a scene with the Englishman getting into one mighty tizzy.

'Calm down old boy,' I said in a cheery tone, the sort that pisses anyone off at the best of times. A few insults followed and I was about to leave the entertainment when the boy from the restaurant arrived. We said nothing, just pressed the button for the elevator. Of course it was broken, so I started to slowly climb the stairs, losing my breath far too quickly. The boy followed two steps behind and just as we arrived to my floor, only five flights up but felt like the height of the Empire State Building, he grabbed my hand with such tenderness that I bit my lip and felt my eyes water.

In closing my door, I hung a sign outside: 'Do not disturb, in the shower.' Ah, someone I thought had a sense humour in these parts.

I found myself shouting: 'Fucking fucks everything up.' I used to resist the cheap attraction of a flirtatious waiter or the common oik winking or sticking his tongue out in a bar but this time I could not resist. To be brutally honest when he asked me in sign language to take off my shirt, I wanted to start rendering the song, *Happy times are here again*. Cheesy I know, but a fine interlude before my head started to fill with barbed wire thoughts about how disgusting this all was: 'Me Clifford Coles sucking the cock of a total stranger.' He was a confident so-and-so, the type that is master of any situation. His legs were slightly in the air as he beckoned me towards him.

'A little too much to drink,' I joked, but he did not understand, instead he mumbled something inaudible. 'Speak up boy,' I ordered, but he said nothing and beckoned me over with his bronzed index finger. Then, moving my body from port to starboard and back again – or is it the other way round? I fucked the creature with the strength and enthusiasm of a sixteen year-old, which might well have been the age of my new found friend. I then whispered in his ear to put his cock up my back passage, which was stupid because his English was so bad, he would hardly know what the hell I was talking about. It reminded me of the story when a foreign student went to his doctor complaining of a stomach pain. The doctor gave the student a pellet and explained 'you should put it up your back passage.' The student did this and returned two days later.

'Feel any better?' asked the doctor.

'I did what you said, but for all the good it did, I might as well have shoved it up my arse.'

Ha bloody Ha. I finished off the whole act with a hearty chortle and a yell from my guts. What followed was the quietness of the dead, a post-coital peace. Here he slept in my arms, head on my shoulder. I looked at him and smiled in a moment of contentment. He had on his face one of those expressions that can only be described as swanlike, graceful, and long necked. The whole act had gently subsided and although there were moments of fun, I felt relieved it was over, over, over, as my brain had begun to tighten and felt it was suffering the bends of decompression.

I was expected before lunch and arrived a little late. When I clambered out of bed that morning, there was no sign of my guest. There would be no morning caressing together, naked under the soft white sheet. No, it was better he disappeared into the morning light; I had time to gather my brain cells.

My good, even jovial, mood evaporated as the taxi weaved through the traffic out of Cannes into the surrounding hills. I had hailed the taxi a few feet away from the hotel. It was a

Mercedes, covered with a stream of bumps probably caused by knocking into the innocent strolling hand in hand along the Croisette. The driver, from Turkish descent, mixed Turkish with poor English. He irritated as soon as I had slumped into his uneven seats. It was the usual 'cabbie' complaint: 'How can I afford to keep my family when I get so little money.' As he moaned the meter was quickly mounting. Once he started to regale about the pitfalls of the French government, I had had enough.

'Shut the fuck up and get me to where I want to go.' At first he looked startled and then let out the deepest sigh. I caught him curse, 'merde', under his breath. I looked at my watch and saw if we did not get moving I was bound to be late. Damn! We had not moved for twenty minutes. 'Get a bloody move on,' I yelled. The driver started to hoot and then everyone joined in a cacophony of sound much like those yob idiots behave when their local team have won a football match. The sweat-stained taxi driver got out of the car and started to curse another driver. I thought for one moment there was going to be a murder; they had their hands round each other's necks. Then quite suddenly the traffic started to move and the noise subsided. The taxi driver stopped his hold, shook his opponent's hand, and returned to the car.

The taxi drew up outside the house, the grandest we had yet passed. 'Take this!' I dropped the exact fare into his chubby hands. 'Now off you go, you miserable git.'

I rang the bell from the black iron wrought gates. There was no answer, the gates simply opened. The air smelt of lemon, the air warm, with a hint of dust.

D had his arms in the air. He was playing football with his father and was celebrating a goal. With his skin bronzed and his hair lightened and a touch long, he looked like a young god praising the sun. The welcome was friendly, even Constance flashed a smile. 'Let's have lunch,' and she grabbed hold of my arm and led me to a long table under a tree. As we walked I felt slightly damp under my armpit. I did not dare to see whether my shirt was wet. It is not acceptable to look hot and flustered at any social occasion even if the night before you had slept on a park bench; that damn taxi driver!

The food was served by Lilly, a Filipino flown over from their home in England. She purred each time she served D and snorted each time she served me. Must have been the shirt I thought.

John fired questions about Falston and regaled some of his prep school stories. I nodded and chuckled at the right time. Constance half coughed an 'I am so bored', and I wouldn't disagree. John is a bore, a kind bore but a bore nonetheless. How had I not noticed this before? D asked for some more melon, Constance admired her fingernails. The family curtains had been drawn; it was difficult to peep inside. I was being entertained by the shadows of their real selves. I heard their voices but not distinctly. The table was swathed in sadness. My imagination filled in what the ears could not hear. Mother and father hardly spoke to each other and poor darling D was left alone to grow. A lousy game of football was no good – that does not make you a father. The wind rustled the trees and the scent of the sea a few miles away met the table. John kept on with his tales. Sssh, ssh, for Christ's sake be quiet. I have to think, I have to protect this boy from the disquiet of his parents. My teachings will be better value than a silly game of football. Then there is a cackle of laughter from D, which breaks my trance. John's story was coming to an end and I followed suit and laughed; Constance was silent. Then the laughter suddenly died and we all started to eat the fish.

Our afternoon walk was to the top of the property, up the hill, a hike if ever there was one, and just as my sweat had dried, it started to fall by the gallon. My heavy breathing would not stop, damn it! My mouth was opening and shutting probably like the fish we had just eaten, caught only a few hours before by an eager fisherman. Constance had retired for a siesta, good on her, and so it was just the three of us; the three men. We were climbing a fucking mountain. Why can't people just relax after a hearty lunch? What is it about a certain type that needs to exercise all the time. Nearly there, nearly there. Why has John made so much money? If he had done less well, he would not have been able to buy this bloody hill. They reached the summit five minutes before I did. All I could see were their feet hovering over the ledge.

'Come on, Coles, I thought you were meant to be the sports master!' Ha bloody ha! Daggers drawn but I let out a hearty laugh. Mosquitoes were out in force up there and I spent my time flapping at their passing sound. John took no notice of them or rather pretended to take no notice, his blood already sucked out of him. I kept slapping my hand against my arms and legs, sometimes catching a little brute so that a squirt of blood burst over my skin – probably my blood. Blood to blood. Dust to dust: 'In the sweat of thy face shalt thou eat bread, till thou return unto the ground; for out of it wast thou taken: for dust thou art, and unto dust shalt thou return.'

How I needed a drink! Preferably water but no one had bothered to bring the bottles from the lunch table.

We started our descent and, to pass the time, I thought of disappearing into the house and taking a concoction of pills in a glass of white wine, it would do the trick. How bedraggled I must have looked in front of D. He of course looked beautiful, the occasional droplet falling from his brow. John went to put his arms round his shoulders as they walked together but D, in a teasing manner, pushed him away and started to race down the hill. Look at him fly, brown limbs stretched and a radiant smile appearing as briefly as sunlight caught on a spider's web swaying in the breeze.

We were reaching the house when D lost his footing and fell to the ground. I started to run to reach him, my tiredness suddenly vanishing. When I put my arm on D's knee to offer him a little sympathy, he shook it off, lifted his head, looked me straight in the eyes and said, 'I am all right now!' I stood glued to the gravel and thought that there could be no doubt he was ready for our next chapter; I would wait for the moment. Everything, they say, is timing.

*   *   *

'It's OK, I'll deal with this,' I kept repeating. I looked at my eyebrows, which suggested that I was not in the mood for any trouble. Stay calm you fool, he will be back soon. I swug a brandy; always a calming effect. Why was I in such a state? Don't most of us react, rather than respond, when we reckon something, or for that matter, anything, which we felt was about to be ours, is about to be taken from us?

I flung my jacket across the chair and ripped the buttons off my shirt. What a child I can be. I was the person that night who moves so quickly, that he could flick the switch off and get into bed before the light was out. I pulled the sheets over my head and tried to calm myself. Stop? I told my mind. I appeased it with fantasies of the head of the Governors taking me to one side and saying, 'We need you, Coles. Take charge of the school. It's asking for a firm hand; you're the only man for the job.' But before I fully calmed down I confessed to my pillow: I do not know what to do next. At last it's 'truth time'! I yelled into my pillow. How I needed to shout and shout I did: 'EVERY-ONE GETS WHAT HE DESERVES.'

*   *   *

D was late returning to school from half term that winter. Poor chap seemed to have caught flu or something, or maybe a resurgence of a dormant bite from one of those fucking mosquitoes.

I missed him as I wandered through those desolate corridors. I had planned to call his home many times but resisted. How considerate the parents would have been to just let me know all was OK, that he was not that sick and I had nothing to worry about. My God people can be so selfish! I questioned myself though: Was I being thoughtful or merely a lustful, irrational drunk? I did not call. Instead I waited and waited without news . . . A voice kept repeating, 'They have stolen him from you.' I fabricated a conspiracy in my midst.

Walking past the games room, I was sniffed by both the headmaster's new labrador and by his wife. The former around my scuffed suede shoes, the latter with her nose firmly in the air. I had not paid much attention to the first lady recently and she had drifted into an almighty sulk. Silly cow! I turned on the charm and regained some lost ground. 'And how are you Mrs Draper? Fine day at last. My, you look well . . . '

'I wonder whether, Mr Coles . . . would you do me a favour?'

My heart plunged, what does the cow want now?

'I have to go into Norwich this evening to hear a recital and will not be able to pick up D from the station. You wouldn't mind . . . would you?'

The question, in truth, took my breath away, a rare excursion into the realm of being stunned.

'We know how close you are to his parents. The father is full of praise. Your name consistently comes up in conversation. Visited them in the South of France I believe? It would be nice for D to have a friendly face to greet him, now wouldn't it? He will be arriving on the 6.10 . . . Good!' With that she walked away, shoulders slumped, disappearing with her puppy being dragged behind. I, in my mind's eye, lifting up a shotgun as if it were a large cock suddenly erect and pointing it to her head 'Bang bang and thank you very much!'

The nights set early in November, never welcoming. The darkened sky loomed over the station and I waited under a light so D could see, as the train drew in, that someone was waiting. I bought a packet of fruit pastilles at the news kiosk, thinking that it would be a pleasant surprise for the boy. The kiosk man was a surly sod.

'Do you have change for a five pound note?' I asked.

'No I don't,' he replied.

I bought a local paper to add to my total. He took my money with a sneer.

'Cunt,' I hissed under my breath, but he did not react. Probably he was used to insults, being a big one to humanity himself.

The train was late and I gave up standing to attention and took a seat on an ugly plastic blue bench on the platform. The local newspaper was banal, except the front page reporting of an escape from the local institution of a grade A sexual offender, whatever the fuck that means. They tend to abscond from jail rather easily. The bold headline of *'Enough is Enough'* is bound to bring more control with security, and no bad thing. A sado-masochist pervert with a conviction for rape and murder on the loose; for Christ's sake, we have children nearby! The irresponsibility of bourgeois bureaucrats, 'Who the fuck do they think they are?' Bored with their own dull, suffocating lives, trying to change people's mentalities rather than control them.

Finally the train arrived, breathing out a groan as it moved slowly into the station. I stopped in my tracks as D jumped off the train, looking straight into his eyes as I welcomed him back. 'Not a blemish,' I said, studying his face carefully and I was right. His face was unmarked by the measles and still as fresh as that April day. He was quiet, but I could see he was relieved to see me.

He lugged a heavy overnight bag and barely threw it into the boot of my car. We drove back to school saying little. It was a Sunday evening like any other Sunday evening, there was hardly a car in sight, and the country lanes belonged to us. He grabbed the sweets that were offered. His breath was firm and the smell of the sweet fruit spilt from his full mouth. I wanted to kiss the boy at the end of his nose, that delicate perfect nose, but I resisted.

Oh, the throbbing of my heart. It was so loud I thought the whole county would have heard. Be still my beating heart, I commanded myself. But my mind had been made up. I would ask D to come to my room that night. I was to wait no more.

'Tonight I will come and fetch you,' I said as he left the car. His face I will never forget. It blanched with a mark of surprise followed by a gauntlet of emotion, finishing with a sense of relief. He said nothing, but I could tell our friendship had finally changed course. Oh ye of little faith! And I heralded our new beginning.

I was on night duty and after the boys knelt to say their prayers, I turned off the lights in each dormitory. The faces of boys so white, a feminine white as they turned to their pillows, falling into their dreams. The gloomiest hours are those waiting minutes. I occupied them with half a bottle of whiskey, a prayer to the day behind and the glorious evening ahead. I chain-smoked a packet of Dunhill and dreamt about what I had waited for, ever since I saw D that early September afternoon four years before. Let's be clear here, my love has never been unnatural. I cared for his well-being, let there be no argument with that. I do not prey on children whom I believe are still at the age of innocence. I looked at my watch, where the hell was he? I would go and fetch him. Before I set forth into his dormitory, I stalled and convinced myself to resist. Yes, resist like Orpheus. He is there, that is all that matters but my urge was too dominant and I felt the latch of my mind click slightly and urge me to move forward; Dear Lord I surrendered.

I whispered, 'Come to my room in ten minutes.' He was asleep. I shook him and he groaned something indistinguishable. 'Hurry up!' I ordered, perhaps a little too forcibly.

I did not have to wait long. Soon there was an uneasy knock on my door. I opened it. I offered him a glass of blood red wine as if there was nothing out of the ordinary. 'To our friendship,' I toasted.

'Thank you,' he said, cross-mouthed and awkward.

'Don't mention it,' I said.

I felt his arm; I shuddered in ecstasy and rubbed his shoulders to gain my equilibrium. D's body glistening from my single light. Oh the delirium of that moment. I pulled free the chord from his pyjamas. God help me . . . How I had prayed for this moment. Prayers work. Again, and again, and again. Voices comforted: 'There are times when you must be selfish.'

*   *   *

'What's wrong?'

D didn't answer.

'Why the tears?'

The headmaster had caned him.

'What did you do?'

'I was caught smoking with Proudlock behind the squash courts.' Strange, he said it in a different tone that jolted a sense of nostalgia, like seeing lambs that are no longer quite lambs. D was growing up, striding towards a new physique, striding towards a new appreciation and joy. I admit I have the deepest feelings for the boy. No feeling have I felt like this before, but I am trying, and I think succeeding, in not having favourites – D will always be the exception to everything in life. But I care for them all. How can our intolerance be against anything except how many of us there are? I had a stern word with myself over the Easter holidays after I cursed at an elderly gentleman for hailing a cab before me. I'd been standing on the street corner in the pissing rain and I lost it. If the elderly man had stopped the cab, he probably would have used the stick he was carrying to wallop me over the head. I had decided to begin a new chapter and try to rid myself of my bad temper; it was time to grow up and to become the man I always wanted to be. I recognised swearing showed a lack of self-restraint . . . fuck it.

'Well, I've heard of greater calamities! Bring Proudlock to my room and I will try to cheer you both up.'

'What, now, sir?'

'Yes, find your friend and I'll be waiting for you.'

D's face hardened and with a mournful tread he went off to find Proudlock.

'Don't dally, be quick!'

The boys arrived soon after I had finished a quick drink, the third of the day. I hid the glass under the bed; I did not want to give the impression that I drink in the afternoon – that would not do.

They shared the same expression; fear glazed in their eyes.

'Wipe away those sad faces,' I ordered. 'What you did is not the end of the world.'

And I pulled out my pack of Rothmans from my top drawer.

'Here take one.' Is this a mad person I saw their eyes yell. They looked quizzically.

'Take it.' I said.

Tentatively they did. The air was suddenly chill. I lit their cigarettes with a Zippo lighter I'd bought on one of my excursions to Norwich. The old trick of one sweep against the leg.

'Enjoying it?' I asked. They did not answer.

'You're smoking it wrong. Watch. Take a deep inhale, hold in the throat like this and release. Inhale . . . deeper, deeper, a lungful and release.' The boys tried and gave the inevitable cough.

'Watch this.' Again, I took a deep drag, pulled the cigarette out of my mouth and released the perfect smoke ring which floated gently in front of the white sunlight bleaching my window.

'Wow,' D exclaimed, his eyes suddenly alive.

'Shall I do it again?'

The boys giggled, 'Yes please, sir!'

And I repeated it with multiple rings floating in to the air. I heard their laughter and groped for the ultimate sense of happiness, how I needed that. I was in paradise until the wail of an ambulance passing nearby shook me out of my stupor. It wailed slowly, knowing there was little hope. So why wail at all?

'Better go boys.' I sensed I was beginning to lose control, pull yourself together Coles. 'But before you leave . . . ' I went to my wash bag and pulled out a bottle of lemon cologne. I began to spray their clothes to cover the smell of smoke.

'Sssh! Not a word to anyone or else we will all be in deep shit,' I said.

How familiar I had become in D's life. How liberating! It was good to see D smile again, he hadn't smiled for a while. I felt a sudden desire. I felt a sudden strong desire . . . I felt a sudden strong desire to ask Proudlock to leave, to leave D alone with me. Jesus, how I loved and hated, how I adored and denied. How I needed and reviled.

'Why do you smoke, sir?' asked Proudlock.

'It keeps my weight down.'

The boys laughed and I laughed, banishing the darkest thoughts from my mind. A large tick by my name. I wanted that afternoon to go on and on, treating each other as equals, no longer the master and student. The boys left the room with the caning a distant memory.

I sank deep into my chair and started a debate in my head whether what I had done was the right thing. I concluded that I am grateful that I see, feel, and trust and practice what I preach. When I run the school, I will do it in my style and not the way tradition dictates.

After a brief doze, I found myself being pulled as if by a magnet to confront the headmaster. His methods were antiquated and he needed to be told. I found him in the staff room looking shifty. He rarely visited and when he did, there was good reason and not a very pleasant one. His face was creased, as if he had been buried in Mrs Draper's boobs for hours. His smell, for no good reason, was horrifying, a body odour resembling a cheese smell of puke. He seemed to have already seen me as I entered, but turned in a suspiciously brisk fashion.

'Excuse me headmaster, do you mind if I talk to you?'

The headmaster stopped, sighed, and instead of hearing what I had to say went on about how difficult it had become to run Falston on his own.

'I need a deputy head,' he said, but then his words became unintelligible, his mind drifting off like a lost vessel. I tried to call him back to the deputy head theme but he was miles away talking about how dirty the town had become, 'litter bloody everywhere,'

'You were talking about the deputy head position, head-master, DEPUTY HEAD . . . '

'Was I? Rather drab outside isn't it?'

The sun glared through the windows.

'Yes, awful weather, headmaster.' I replied.

I had sought the headmaster with an objective to tell him

that the use of the cane was outdated; instead I ended up sitting on the fence. If you're going to sit on the fence Mr Coles, sit on it firmly. One day you may discover that the fence has been pulled down and – shock of horror – someone has taken your place. At that moment of contemplation, the geography master strolled in.

'Good afternoon, headmaster, I hope I'm not disturbing you?' he fawned.

'Of course not,' the headmaster replied.

*   *   *

I rocked in my bed, gently waiting for the sun to come up properly. I drank a shot of whiskey before brushing my teeth – the naughty pleasure of it. I drank it slowly, savouring it, meeting it like the morning sun with a smile on my face.

It was the biennial trip to Burford to see how our boys matched with theirs. I was taking the geography master for company. He was mighty flattered that he was chosen. Up came the sun. Was the sun early or was my alarm late? I did not care as I felt excitement about the prospect of leaving our little world, even if it was for just the two days. I always had a yearning for Oxford and cheered by the fact that the city would be nearby. I would like to one day make it my home. Where the young meet with the old buildings. Perfect for my appetite. A friend of a friend's friend offered me a first job to teach a bunch of gormless rich foreigners. It was pompously called The Oxford School of the English Language. 'When the young spoke English proper . . . ' was their slogan. As Mark Twain described, 'The minimum sound to maximum sense.' Oh God it sounded awful, so I turned down the chance to ask lads to repeat tongue twisters like: 'The cute acolytes swing thurifers as furiously as Thor.' It probably would not ever have reached that stage. All you would have to do was teach

121

the boy to say 'Yes please,' 'No thank you,' 'Fuck me,' and bingo, the father hands over the cheque.

The cricket team waited in the drive with overnight bags slung over shoulders. Bloody late as usual, the awful local coach company. Eventually an old man of a driver drove up wearing a busman's cap.

'Think I am too old for the job?' he said, as if he had read my mind.

'No, not at all,' I replied, 'you can't be a day over eighty.'

'Think I am too old for the job don't you?' he repeated.

Oh dear, the old boy's senile.

'Doctor, doctor, I am worried about my memory.'

'How long has it been like that?'

'How long has what been like that.'

This could be a long drive. I decided I would sit close up front with map in hand.

The boys were excited and cheered at the prospect of the hundred-mile journey. Even D, whose mood I could never guess, giggled at a lame joke from the boorish Asquith. Our friendship was like a game of chess, mapped out and played up to a certain crucial point, and then left to gather the first fall of dust.

I gave the team a pep talk for the long trip and coming weekend, with quotation and misquotation from the Second World War, which most were studying for their Common Entrance Examination: 'We want to get the hell over there. The quicker we clean up this goddamned mess, the quicker we can take a little jaunt against the purple-pissing Japs and clean out their nest, too. Before the goddamned Marines get all of the credit.' The boys looked confused, but after four hours in the coach they will get the idea.

'How shall I treat them today?' I asked myself. Like a summer holiday? I decided to be relaxed and avoid any sudden mood swing. I have a flask tucked into the inside pocket of my suit, just in case.

D was silent most of the journey, but his eyes spoke loudly even above the tuneless hum of the boys singing. When we paused at a shitty motorway café, I noticed D was not eating.

'Eat young man,' I said in a loving way, and he looked sad whilst he finished his plate of sausages and fries. I do think I love him but he remains too young to fulfil my definition of what love is: being able to confide in someone, and to know that despite all your confessions, they still take you in, still listen to more, take you, warts and all; till the time comes when you ache so painfully that you can't be without him or her. Love is saying 'I love you', and the other believing it, although knowing full well it is complete bullshit. The repetition of this debate hammers in my head every day. I am beginning to think love may well be out of my reach this time round.

By the time we reached the monstrosity of a building, the lull of the last hour washed away and cheers welcomed our arrival. A modernistic carbuncle built after an arson attack by some aristocrat who, as rumours went, was corrupted by pornography – the link between pornography and setting a building on fire, I am still trying to work out. As for me, I do not want to see a lot of rape, drug-taking, fornication and homosexuality in a magazine – I see enough of that in my quarters.

We were greeted by Rev. Watkins, the cricket master and school chaplain. He was a spindly little man so weak that a hug hello could crush him slowly to a pulp. A man so clean that I reckoned he scrubbed his hands each time he had finger-tipped another human, and whose aftershave had a faint scent of nail polish. He stepped forward and offered a wet fish of a handshake welcoming us to Burford. I shook it and backed away with chills in direct contrast to the warm temperature. He looked extremely camp. The types these prep schools employ! It was the first time we met. I did not bother to ask what had happened to his predecessor, Mr Wallace; thought it was always impertinent to ask why or where an ex-teacher has disappeared to. I introduced the geography master and the two shuffled away in conversation.

I led the boys to the cricket field to get some fresh air and to inspect the square. I admit a far superior pitch to ours. It was surrounded by sun-kissed grass and right along the boundary were oak trees. The air hung with the aroma of fresh mown grass, ice cream and homemade sponge cakes. The long journey instantly evaporated and the eyes of the boys awakened with a voice of desire to avenge last year's defeat. 'This is the perfect place to play with your heart,' I pleaded to the boys and I felt their ambition saturate the atmosphere.

Like all good things in life, the good mood was bankrupted by something ugly and uninviting. The headmaster's wife sidled herself between us. A woman with her hair dyed red and nails filed in a pencil sharpener.

'I will take the boys to the gymnasium. That is where they will be sleeping.'

Oh, dear God, mix me a clap of thunder and rid me of people like this! Mrs Longford Smith Milne-Hedges, would you believe it? – walked the obedient boys away, laughing like a horse. A quadruple barrel name she had probably craved for all her life. As yet the headmaster was nowhere to be seen. Probably died years ago, but no one had bothered to tell neither the school nor his wife.

I called out to the geography master who was still talking to his new best friend; it was time to follow me to our sleeping quarters. It turned out to be a plain room with a single hanging light in the middle of the ceiling. Two beds not as yet pushed apart, which I did as soon as I caught sight of the faux pas. It had the air of being like the room of a Bangkok brothel I visited two years previously. I am proud to say that I was invited as a VIP in through the back door. Perhaps that is my definition of success; being allowed in the back doors of brothels throughout the world.

I poured a hearty shot of whiskey into a clean glass, which miraculously was left on the table. 'Here, have one too.' He drank in a gulp and I poured some more.

'Look what I have.' The geography master delved into his bag and brought out a bottle of vodka. We laughed like naughty schoolchildren . . . I grabbed for it and he slapped my hand with force, like a piano lid falling on it. 'Later,' he ordered. Shit, he is even beginning to boom like me. Before I left to join the boys outside for a barbecue/picnic, I heard a sound from my stomach.

'Christ what was that?' I cried.

'Sounded like a tank back-firing,' the geography master replied.

I was sweating profusely, so much so I believed I was going to shrivel up.

'Have another shot of whiskey,' the geography master unwisely advised.

Bastard wants to be rid of me. But I took his suggestion. Down it went and the shock sparked a miraculous recovery. I wet my face in the sink opposite, changed my shirt, and regained my composure. I walked outside with the poise of a man conducting a military band; mind you, not a good military band, bum note following bum note. By the time I joined the picnic, I was conducting a national anthem with shoulders back and hand stretched out confidently.

'How do you do, my name is Coles, so pleased to be here this fine summer evening. May I introduce the geography master . . . ' The headmaster had finally made a guest appearance. He eyed me suspiciously, don't they all these days? He acted like a conductor who can direct his symphony orchestra without score; I almost applauded his performance.

The boys seemed to be getting on, hurried talk about what school they would be going on to. I was thinking of death, ignoring the boorish conversation of fellow masters. 'Shut up will you,' I wanted to shout. These swings are becoming unbearable, only a second before I was ready to take on the world, then there was a sudden feeling of despair. I don't mind where I die; I just don't want to die alone. Preferably not meet my enemy in a lonesome hospital bed in a far off corner of the world, with the stench of piss filling my nostrils and soaking my sheets. Perhaps I won't die in a flash but draw it out like a cockroach, who after being stamped on fifty times, still moves some part of its body. But I swear I will not panic; was any man ever the happier for being unhappy about death and did he live any longer? I shall face my maker as I am. I shall not try to impress the Almighty like a schoolboy who has left it too late for the exam and stays up all night only to meet the examiner the next meeting in a state of collapse. No, my life will be viewed from my first breath to my last. The whole pudding, all the ingredients, and if it is decided I be sent below, let that be God's will. But I am not a bad man and have done more good than evil. Beware of the devil in sheep's clothing, there are many about. They are charming, amusing and primarily evil. Beware, for you know whom I talk about? And my skin crawls just remarking upon it!

And then suddenly from the far end of the field, emerges part of my salvation. D had walked away from the pack with a member of the opposition and was returning to the group, a large Oak shadowing each of their steps. Where had they been? I cared not. He looked contented which lifted my gloom. Ah that mood swing. Welcome!

As the boys moved away, I beckoned D over and told him to

report to my room after all were asleep. He gave no reaction other than a nod of the head. 'Did you hear me?' I raised my voice.

'Yes, sir,' he replied. Good, I did not want insubordination.

The head's wife took charge in putting our boys to bed.

'You can leave it to me,' she had ordered. I did not argue even though I felt it was my responsibility. God, I hoped I would never run into her again. If ever in the future I glimpsed that dragon coming towards me in the street, I would slink at once into the doorway of a shop and hold my breath until she was out of sight.

It was eleven o'clock when I heard distant strides on the steps leading to our room. How quickly one can recognise a sound so close to one's heart. D arrived as we were drinking, and we had been drinking far too much; I was drunk. Maybe it was the alcohol that created the perception of fear that swept through D's body like pins pushed under fingernails.

I refuse to go into the detail of the night, other than remark on how the geography master had turned from, at first, being someone fearful, to someone who shrieked triumphantly when the deed was done.

'It will ruin my career,' he had ached before and after. Huh, his career! There is no career there, Mr Geography. It will only be later that the broader issues will haunt you. He was reaching the point of someone ready to refute the existence of a soul, let alone possess one himself. Yes, it was that phase of the journey. Witnessing him with D was like a death in the family, like having a father whom you seldom see or appreciate but you know is there, and being suddenly told he refuses to see you at his deathbed. The Jesuits were right: get a child young enough, and however much he retreats to what he has been taught, he will never completely escape. For this happened to me, you see, do you understand? There had been no treasure at the end of the fairy tale. The mark was set before I was eight, the cut so deep that I felt comfortable if only I massaged it.

*　　*　　*

I felt like a horse the next morning, bowing its head into the bag eating its oats but with ribs exposed more numerable with each hour – exposing guilt, fear, and loneliness. I had awoken from a dreamless sleep. Perhaps it was the act of the night before, watching instead of participating, or maybe it was the intake of cheap booze mixed with the geography master's vodka. I had bought a cheap bottle of whiskey at the off-licence during our motorway stop. Forgot the basic rule: the cheaper the booze, the more lethal its bite, like snakes: the smaller the snake, the bigger the bite.

The boys ate their breakfast in a manner as if, back at Falston, they were not fed. 'More sausages?' offered the cook.

'Yes please.'

What an eager group they are. Not only hungry for food but also hungry for victory. After breakfast we all attended chapel. The sleeping bags had been cleared and replaced by steel chairs. The masters and their families sat in the two front rows. Rev. Watkins greeted me with a feigned Sunday smile and gently nodded his head; a sinking feeling came over me as when a Priest announces how much more of his sermon there is to follow. I sat with arms resting on my knees, my shirt damp under my light blazer, my heart pounding. I noticed the geography master's face; he looked tired and he looked removed. His eyes resembled how I suspect a terrorist looks as he straps a bomb to his waist. Little bastard had been nagging for the introduction, so to speak, and when finally his continual harassment worked and I relented, there had not been a moment of recognition. Didn't he realise that this was the greatest gift I could give?

I felt bereft. I grieved. Nothing would be the same again. In fact, nothing will be again. My aim was to move forward at the same pace as time, and there, paradoxically, hardly notice it.

'Our Father, who art in heaven, hallowed be thy name . . . ' I bellowed out the Lord's Prayer, partly to fill in a new silence and partly to alleviate the slight, if crazy, fears, popping in and out of my head nudging me towards insanity; I will never forgive the geography master. The game started at twelve so that we would be able to leave in good time to miss the damn traffic. We won the toss and decided to bat, and bat we did. D hit the ball with gusto and the relief of a wicked child who got away with murder. He struck the ball with such wonder that he became a man in front of my very eyes. Striking and smacking it to every corner of the glorious boundary, breathing through his mouth, head down. What an innings, what a show! 115 not out from a total 148 for 5.

'Finest innings I have ever witnessed from a young man,' I bleated out at our early tea and everyone nodded in agreement. We bowled the opposition out for a paltry forty-six runs. Ha! They were torn apart after our triumphant innings. We tasted blood, attacked, and left the wounded animal to lie dying in the middle of the road.

I issued a brief end of game statement to masters and parents: 'Thank you for your hospitality and for the fine weather. We look forward to welcoming you next year. We wish you every success with the rest of your season.' A patronising but sympathetic tone to finish my speech. And then, without warning, I had a vision of ants gorging at the underbelly of an overturned beetle. A slug crushed by the foot of a startled hare. I yearned for a drink to rid me of these darkened thoughts. 'Need to go the toilet, be right back.' I hurried to the bathroom before swigging at my flask; a look round to make sure no one was watching. Salvation and a

129

sweep of sedation greeted the rest of the day and our tiresome journey home.

The coach that picked us up had a different driver for the return journey; perhaps the old boy had died during the night. I gave the replacement quite a shock by grabbing his elbow and pulling him towards me: 'Where's the old boy?' I asked, genuinely concerned.

'He did not feel well, so he took to his bed.'

'Send him my best won't you?' I insisted and let go of his elbow. I turned my face fully towards the sky. The sun remained strong and quietly I congratulated myself for being so thoughtful.

The journey home swept by and we reached Cromer as the light had almost gone and we were past the exact moment at which dusk can be said to have ended and night to have begun.

'A commemoration of your beautiful innings young man,' I handed the day's cricket ball to young D as the coach turned into the school's drive. He accepted, it not with grace, but mournfully, eyes not meeting mine. 'What could be wrong with the dear child?' This should be one of the best days of his life yet his face had turned grey and his eyes resembled his mother's scorn. I promised to have a quiet word with him.

*   *   *

The week that followed was slow and painful. Only last night I caught D gazing at me with a sense of disbelief and bewilderment. There was something truly amiss; he acted like a dog aware of an earthquake, uneasy on his feet, unsure of his next step. I should have been more conscious than to bring someone else into our secret. What a fool I had been! With hindsight, with the beauty of hindsight. Yes, because of hindsight so much is so obvious.

'Come and see me later,' I stage-whispered across the table.

My dear God, I managed to sound so loud. I was beginning to lose my mind. I had to leave the racket of the dining room to breathe in some air and offer myself words of comfort. My, it did not last long. I was soon scolding and belittling myself for being such a fool, banging my head again, again with my right palm. 'FOOL, FOOL, FOOL,' I repeated.

'Are you all right, sir?' asked the head of school with a broad smile across the face of a bumptious schoolboy, going to collect prizes galore for the classics, long jump, and logarithms.

'I am fine boy, I will be in . . . in . . . in a second'

I took out a pipe and a leather pouch from my blazer pocket, pressed some tobacco down into the pipe, extricated a match from a matchbox, lit the match, then the tobacco all with one hand. I turned and smiled at the ghost of my father that I imagined was standing beside me as I executed the intricate manoeuvre. I had found my father's pipe the previous evening whilst rummaging through an old suitcase. I thought it would make me look more distinguished, statesman-like, a man waiting for his destiny.

I took a single puff of the pipe and for an instant tasted my dead father. I did neither choke nor wretch, instead I enjoyed my peace until the boy interrupted.

'We are waiting to say grace, sir.'

'I am coming damn you!'

I hit the bell as if at the 'test of strength' stall. This time there would be no prize, just a pregnant silence as the boys with their heads down joined in my lead for grace. 'For what we have received may the Lord make us truly thankful. AMEN.'

The over enthusiastic chemistry master took over the night's duty of making sure all boys completed their prep.

'Have a wonderful night, Mr Coles,' he said, in the most accommodating tone. And for one of those fleeting moments, I felt a surge of bliss waft through my veins; the tiptoe of pure thoughts that it was good to be alive and my life was heading forward, onward and upward. Funny how that happens when you are in the midst of a deep gloom. I decided to mark 2A's homework in the staff room, which was thankfully empty. My red pen was at the ready and when I started to read the one on the top of the pile, it was so badly written and constructed that I began to descend back into my hole and question my ability as a teacher. I felt a fake, a phony, like someone who had his first book accepted, or shall we be kind and call it a 'novel', and when left alone in the publisher's office, happened to glance down on the editor's desk and notice a letter which he picked up and looked at, only to discover it was from his very own mummy and daddy who have said in the letter that they will 'foot all the bills for the book's publication, promotion, distribution, PR, party, and its probable losses on the understanding our child is never told'.

'You look tired,' said the headmaster's wife, peering her head round the door.

'Just finishing off marking 2A's history.' It is easy to feel good when feeling good, but downright fucking impossible to feel good when feeling bad; the headmaster's wife was certainly not going to alter my mood.

'Looking for someone, Mrs Draper?'

'Perhaps it is you I am looking for Mr Coles.'

I lowered my head so as not to meet her eyes. Only last term she had invited herself back into my room and started preaching: 'I think we should all die without guilt in our hearts don't you Mr Coles? I am thinking that I should admit our tryst to the headmaster.' The next thing I remembered was her hand disappearing into my flies. 'You are so damn attractive, Mr Coles, you know you are.' I needed a drink before facing my next fate; my job was on the line for Christ's sake!

'Sherry?' I asked. She did not answer, so in desperation I started to recite a lesson from my former English teacher at public school: 'When you are confused, put all your old beliefs in a cardboard box on top of your tallest wardrobe and leave them there. Make a fresh start. The old ones are always available, if you want or need them, or they can gather dust while you discover what are for you, greater truths.'

'Stop talking crap, Mr Coles,' and she hopped, skipped and jumped, crashing us to the floor. Part of me screamed and not from my mouth, and a horrible hollow appeared in the pit of my stomach as if I had been winded. I held my breath and prayed it would all end, as I imagined stifled laughter on the other side of the door. This was rape for God's sake, and I cursed the sheer audacity of her perverted behaviour. Considering the circumstances, and let's not forget she was performing her act in a room where anyone could walk in, I felt my silence showed a tremendous amount of loyalty to the school. I mean if I had gone straight to the headmaster or better still a governor, there would have been hasty resignations.

Mrs Draper and I had become nodding acquaintances since then and throughout the summer term; it hadn't been until this moment that we had traded words.

Her voice suddenly lowered, it had a certain spooky, yet seductive clarity to it, 'I know you are up to no good Mr Coles, I sense it. I simply don't know what it is. Perhaps you are having an affair with some tart in town?'

I managed a croak as a reply and then she continued.

'That abused washer girl for instance who comes into the school to help with the laundry. She was mouthing off about how attractive you are. I overheard her say, "The handsome Mr Coles gives me the odd wink as he passes by." Screwing her, Mr Coles, is that why you have been avoiding me?'

No Mrs Draper, sometimes when we hang something so hideous on the wall we soon learn to tolerate it, like it, even love it. We grow and our views grow with us. Our attitudes alter, and ought to. But with you Mrs Draper, I still retain the view I had from our very first meeting. I want to eradicate from my mind everything that reminds me of you but it seems I cannot forget. You are everything I fear, a bad taste in the mouth, suffering toothache, suffering insomnia, famine, electrodes fixed to my balls, cancer, haemorrhoids and food poisoning, listening to the news, puking from a lonely bed, sleeping in the street. Consider yourself included in this list. It is the opposite of when I love someone and unhappiness disappears as lightly as a moth out of a night window. I fantasise of all good things in life; as when a jet flies over suburbia on a summer's day, lying under bed blankets shining a torchlight, enjoying the smell of bread, listening to ice cubes hitting the edge of the freshly cut summer grass. Get on your knees Mrs Draper, and while you are down there, you might as well pray.

I heard Mrs Draper shout. She was repeating her question. 'Are you screwing her?' I paused. I looked up. I stood up. I looked down at the marked essays. I was looking for something to bind them together. I found a large elastic band. That would do. Mrs Draper shouted again, she wanted an answer. I ignored her. I had an appointment to make. 'Mr Coles, I am talking to you.'

I ignored her once again. I AM IN A HURRY. I AM LATE. WE ARE ALL TOO LATE. IT IS TOO LATE. I wished her good-night.

The school was peaceful. I looked into one of the dormitories. The boys were silent as statues. I walked from bed to bed. This was the most junior dormitory, boys as young as seven. I picked up a teddy bear from the floor and tucked it back into a

134

boy's bed. I heard his breath, a stuttered sound through his nose. I managed to stay silent, even with my eyes, but my mind was screaming, 'Get to your room, D will be waiting.' I sat on the edge of the bed. I was unsure of his name; it had been his first term. He turned for a moment and gave a beautiful smile. I stroked his hair and turned. 'Be safe now,' I whispered.

D was not waiting. I was going to take the plunge, admit that I had done wrong and for the first time in my life ask for forgiveness. Go on, dive in Coles, or at least jump but I knew I needed a light push to reveal my vulnerability.

There was no knock, D walked trance-like in to my room. I was sitting on the bed. He said nothing, simply began to take off his pyjama top with no sound; simply behaving as if he knew what was expected and acted accordingly. I brushed away some dandruff that had fallen onto my jacket and felt as if I was at my own memorial service. My life was flashing by, my mistakes outweighing the accumulation of regret.

'What are you doing?'

D did not answer but instead, continued to undress.

'Stop!'

D stood still, unsure what to do next, the rosary above my bed clicked regularly against the wall. I mumbled. D did not seem to listen, his lips trembled. Dear God, how I wanted to confess and cry out, 'Father, forgive ME, for I know not what I do – Luke 23:34.' SORRY, SORRY, SORRY, SORRY! This poor drunkard fool, he learnt the hard way the great spiritual lesson of detachment from neurotic desire.

D paused, then said finally, very softly, 'Do you want me to return to my dormitory, sir?'

No, I want you to spend the night, to sleep together naked, caressing each other through the long hours. For you to hear my words that I love you, that I wish your dreams come true and that tomorrow and tomorrow and tomorrow you will believe that I have only meant right by you, that my desire is pure.

'Yes. Go to bed, I'm too tired. It has been a tiring day.'

*　　*　　*

'Sir, sir!' It was a grubby little boy that broke the news, picking his nose with one hand, the other in his pocket. 'The headmaster wants to see you now.'

Instinctively I knew something was wrong. Immediately a deluge of sweat seeped into my shirt, onto my suit. Before going, I had to make a decision: to change into dry clothes, or not to change into dry clothes? My first little dilemma of that morning; yes, I would change. I needed to be confident, preferably be in peak form, in order, zealously, even zestfully, to deal with the accusations that were about to be thrown; for I knew, I just knew what was about to happen. So I went to my room, gave my body a quick rub down, changed into the lucky pumpkin suit and made my way or rather, strolled whistling to his office.

I knocked at the old man's door. 'Come in!' The headmaster was sitting upright in his chair, upright like a judge about to pass sentence; no black hanky on his head, which by all rights there should have been. Something was bound to go wrong over this whole mess of flirtation with the students. How can something so glorious be frowned upon? Did I not teach them well, allow them to digest the knowledge of our history into their minds and stomachs?

His face told that something was on his mind, several things on his mind. I was sitting in an office so familiar but which was now so unfamiliar. I had thought the heavy curtains were crimson, but were now a sick green, blue even. Sweltering hot . . . sweat began again to fall over the brow, 'Sorry I don't know what you are talking about headmaster . . . '

'You swine! Pig! Pack your things and leave, leave these

136

grounds at once . . . I will have to clear the mess after you.' He yelled, and then calmed.

'Am I allowed to defend myself headmaster . . . ?'

The heat was unbearable and in mid-sentence he turned to switch on the fan; one click, two clicks and then to the maximum that made no difference, as the damn thing had never worked.

'Out,' he spat. 'I want you . . . you . . . you . . . off the school grounds within the hour!' And then, as if by a miracle, the fan started to splutter into action and caused a light breeze to fall over the room. Papers ruffled from his desk and some flew into my direction where, with extraordinary instinct, I grabbed them with one hand. No applause though from my audience, just a crumpled face of scorn.

The head was more nervous than me. At one stage he grabbed a knife he used for opening the mail and jabbed it in my direction. Hands shaking, he thumped it into the desk and moaned. Who was in more pain here? He didn't have the guts to take a swing to my body; he was too much of a coward for that.

'Calm down, headmaster. Pour yourself a drink.' I spoke in broken French, much like he had done in the past, 'Pour yourself a drink, headmaster.'

He went to his drinks trolley, didn't hesitate and started to pour himself a sherry. I thought that his heart would burst through his chest. His ticker was so loud; I believed I heard the sound of tick-tock, tick-tock.

Careful, my dear headmaster, we don't want any unfortunate accident now do we? He gulped his drink down in one and then moved his neck, stiff as if it had been underwater for a long time.

'That's better . . . !' he said half choking, finger shaking and pointing to the door. 'Although I want to tear you apart and cut out the perversity that lies within you and swab the decks of your mind, I will not even try. You and I will be the only people from the school to be aware of what has happened. The situation

137

will stay strictly between us. Is that understood?' I fidgeted, knowing that half the school knew already. 'This school is more important than you and if it leaks out that we have had a pervert in our midst, the school would suffer and may eventually shut down. Whatever has happened, it does not deserve that.'

Are we born with a conscience? Is morality taught or caught? Should morality be taught or caught or both or neither?

I was for a moment quite taken aback by the headmaster's speech. At last, the man had shown some guts, good old-fashion disdain. How wrong he was with his assessment, but I was not going to debate that. It was like he read an entire book, left out the important chapters, and had read it backwards.

I think I was with him for five minutes, no more. It was the drink that lengthened the ordeal. At one stage I wanted to offer some pounds to see if I could remain on the school premises until I found suitable accommodation.

'I could book into the Sea View Hotel, headmaster, but I would very much like to remain here with all my belongings . . . '

It is difficult to alter people's mentalities in the twinkling of one argument. The trouble is that they have lived for a long time with what they will call 'goodness', 'tradition' and 'discipline' – which I see as prejudice, ignorance and narrow-mindedness. What the eye does not see, the heart cannot know . . . and all that. There are plenty of ways of being together without official consent. Turn a blind eye, like so many in your position. What do they say; if you leave 'evil' (your term for it) alone long enough it will eventually and inevitably go away. Let's keep this a secret, headmaster, just between us. Imagine the thrill of it, a double secrecy: my secrecy for doing it, your secrecy at suspecting that it is being done. An element of criminality can be splendidly erotic don't you think?

As I was about to leave his office, he suddenly turned and asked, 'You have never thought of suicide have you?'

In order to avoid the answer, I found myself asking another, which subsequently appeared out of nowhere in my head: 'Or murder?'

The headmaster's eyes flashed at me like those of an old iguana disturbed, but next he sighed, indeed much as one imagines an old iguana sighs, and said, 'You better leave now.'

Confusion, hurried steps, boys half-laughing, half-smiling, whispering but not obvious, not too loud – as if we were in church. I held my head high though. I turned the corner close to the staff room and I bumped directly into D. The universe was watching. He looked at me, like seeing a clock that started to work after years being set to the same time. I wobbled – balance, balance!

'WHAT DID YOU SAY? WHY? WHY?' I asked, my confidence suddenly draining from my body, 'I have been your friend. How could you turn on me like this? You who had shared my bread and lifted your heel against me.' I raised my voice, misquoting the Bible.

He said nothing, nothing he said and paced along the corridor, like walking on an uneasy train. How I wanted him to flutter his eyelashes but instead, he was damned by stifled resentment. Our meeting was too quick but still enough time to reach the conceited conclusion that his need to be rid of me was greater than my love.

All I could think of was a drink. Only twenty paces to my room, then five. Just before I opened the door, I saw Proudlock. He also said nothing; instead he picked up his pace as if I were a leper. How the news had spread through the school grapevine. I had to pack, wrap up my picture; those are surely the longest hours, like returning to a lover's apartment to clear out your clothes for the last time. But first things first; I poured and downed in one, poured again and this time it deadened the pain. The mock confidence drained from my eyes, the relief followed by the betrayal and a quiet moment of contemplation. I felt like a dumb man with no voice to speak of my problems, an armless man with no hands to gesticulate . . . I felt impotent of everything I had worked for. The pain dug into me like thorns into Christ. I crossed myself and began to kneel, a prayer at this time, a confession even? I saw a crucifix hanging from my wall. I hadn't noticed it for I don't know how long, probably from the day I returned from a friend's wedding in Mexico City. 'Buy here and be rescued from evil.'

Within a few minutes I was washing my face under a cold tap, sprucing myself up with the cheap lemon aftershave I had bought the previous week. I began to improve. How quickly things change. But then there was a knock, not heavy, slight even. Like knocking and hoping that no one was there. It must be D I thought and, like an excited child, I called, 'Come in!' But the figure standing in the frame of the door was that of the geography master, eager – and that is being kind – to know if his name had been brought up in my conversation with the headmaster.

'NO!' I said, 'Why should it have been?'

'I will pray for you,' said the geography master, but then again who prays for anyone but himself.

I asked him to send on my things which didn't amount to much – picture, books and record player to my sister. He hesitated, probably because for now it would be dangerous to be associated with me, fraternising with the enemy. But don't you realise, you are the enemy Mr Geography!

'Goodbye,' I offered my hand and then whispered some advice in his ear, 'Watch your step!' He was mournful and slouched away. I turned one last time to my room and thought how small it was; I removed the cross and slipped it into my pocket. The quiet closing of the door behind represented the gentle hammering of a distant nail into an as yet unseen coffin.

I had decided to stay at my sister's for the night. Then I would call my friend in Oxford to see if that job was still available. Teaching thick foreigners how to write English; how the mighty fall.

I did not pass a single boy as I stepped out of the school for the last time. It was as if they had been ordered to stay in their classrooms until I left. The fresh air felt fresher than ever before. I refused to up my pace; I was going to walk slowly and with pride. I looked back and caught sight of Mrs Headmaster peeping from the curtain on the first floor; hooked nose and pigtails, the claws of a witch knocking on the windowpane. She would probably scratch my eyes out if we met again, followed by folding back the sheets of her marital bed. How dare she sneer! Soon she will be propped up by pillows surrounded by different shapes, and sized bottles carrying various ointments and pills. She will at first deny using any of them: 'they're only there just in case of a minor ailment!', but weeks will follow where she will give up pretence and cram her avaricious mouth with an assortment of concoctions. *Yummy, yummy, slow death to you* . . .

I turned to face the gate and to face the walk to the station, away from this chapter forever. Before I left the school grounds I thought of D. How he caressed and cared for my body and how extraordinary it was to be looked at by those heavenly eyes, even in the dark.

Why did he betray me? What caused him to confess? Now I presumed others would join the chorus of disapproval . . . daggers still sharp, each and every master with their carnal desire to make fulsome love to those they teach.

PART TWO

TWENTY YEARS LATER

My face resembled the gargoyles hanging over the Bodleian Library, such gnarls and knobs and furrows; faces of chaotic angles and questioned expressions. Mine looked the same, from day to day. I was older, but none the wiser.

Like so many people in mourning, I was trying to make amends. I felt guilty that I had not seen my sister for over a year before her death. She had been loyal after my dismissal from Falston. She sneered at the accusations as pure jealousy. 'The headmaster could see you were after his job' and how right she was! 'They will miss you' she had said; hear, hear! Recently, she had started to materialise in my waking hours. I would stir slowly and my eyes would focus gradually on the lamp to the side of my bed or on some face with a familiar smile; it was the face of my sister. I'd pull up the sheets, wait a moment, peep out quickly and she would still be there. After a while her pale face did not bother; it was a comfort as in finding an old photograph of a loved one left in a book.

I decided to ask my nephew up to Oxford for dinner; Sean had turned into a rather fine creature and I always had a fondness for him. We spoke generally on the last Sunday of each month, and our conversation like many conversations of my day, was dominated by the theme of death. Sean voiced the opinion that afterlife was 'a huge lie invented by those who want to ensure they have dominion of us in this life.' I never challenged his 'platitudinising'. I simply listened and completed my crossword as he warbled on.

Our dinner was interspersed with the spasmodic rumble of thunder threatening to break the warm weather. The heat had hung over the city for months and the collective prayers of the nation, for at least a little break in the weather, seemed to be answered as we were about to order the pudding. The rain fell and roared like Niagara, so much so that we got up from the table and went to the window to see the action outside. It was there that we could see the strength of the rain. It was there we were delivered our after-dinner entertainment. A figure rushed by dressed in black with clothes drenched and collar pulled up to his ears as a form of protection. He was like an undertaker late for a funeral. I sighed at the impression. A loving couple skipped between the puddles that had quickly formed. They were holding hands, now and again having to let go as they jumped different ways.

'Brandy?' I asked. He did not hesitate, his face unusually red, his cigarette smoke evaporating into the baroque ceiling of the restaurant.

He took the glass from my hand, a slight touch of skin.

'Thank you, uncle. To your health and God bless mum.'

His words plunged straight into my heart. We had already demolished two bottles of wine, each in turn filling the other's glass. He looked so much older, quite suddenly he looked like a man, a handsome young man. The shoulders, which were always his defining feature, had broadened. His hands, although he did little manual work, had always had the impression of working in the fields from morning to dark. Thick fingers, nails cut short, a whole hand like a bunch of bananas whenever he picked up his glass of wine. They had strength, unlike my body, which had progressively slumped; the drooping of my joints like running paint. We finished up and stepped out into the rain. If I hadn't known it was rain falling from his face, I would have sworn that my nephew was weeping. The sight was strangely moving. I went to hug him, to give him that reassurance. I took a step forward and then retreated, I knew myself too well.

'What time is your train?' I asked.

'We have half an hour,' he replied. We decided to walk to the station as the rain had ceased and the heat had begun to return; a bit of exercise was not going to do any harm. The walls of the city whispered as we walked by, the few cars injected fuel into the hot air and even St Giles, broad as an overweight aunt, heaved at the smell of pollution. The walk towards Worcester was so familiar that I was beginning to notice nothing except my uneasy breath and the bead of sweat that fell from my brow onto my white shirt. I was about to drum up conversation when my nephew gave me quite a shock, grabbing me by the elbow and pulling me towards him.

'I am glad you are here for me uncle,' I coughed and turned my head. The muscles on his face tightened; it was as if he was about to reveal something that would be too much for my ears. The street was all silent and still. I felt embarrassed. Let's keep walking, I thought.

'Uncle, there is something that I have always wanted to ask ever since . . . '

If I held my breath any longer, I would have fainted. Take the plunge my boy.

'Why were you sacked from Falston? I was young at the time and remember mother and father discussing it, or should I say squabbling. I used to sit on the landing and try to hear what was being said.'

I looked at his face. I saw as soon as he had finished that he had mustered courage to ask the question. There is no justice in the world, thought I: some people succeed without even trying, whilst others . . .

'I was set up by an envious fellow master who realised that I was about to be asked . . . ' You can let go of my elbow now dear nephew; the fourth button of his shirt undone to tantalise, ' . . . to be headmaster, the youngest ever headmaster at Falston.'

He stood in the moonlit silence as if waiting for some word of truth, but none came.

'What happened?' he asked.

I took a deep breath and for an instant, hesitated; it was as if all my thoughts had been pressed to the sides of my brain. 'I was falsely accused of interfering with one of the boys.' It sounded like court charges: 'You, Clifford Coles of Falston School, Norfolk, is hereby formally charged with the sexual assault of a minor. What is your plea, guilty or not guilty? Not guilty, forever not guilty your honour!'

He did not look convinced and I became irritated. I felt his sense of disdain.

'And you?' I asked briskly, in order to turn the spotlight away and to rid myself of any unwanted thoughts. 'Have you ever been falsely accused of something that you were plainly innocent of?' Cool it Coles, my steps in the fallen rain faltered.

'No!' My nephew replied, shrugging his shoulders.

'Well, lucky you!'

I should have laughed the question off, 'Ha ha, one of those things! Typical! We all make mistakes!' But instead, I had blown it with my pissed-off reply. I had the sense, after that, to try to change the subject and discuss my dear sister. I learnt early that once you have blown it, drop the subject as graciously and quickly as possible and leave. On no account try to explain, cover up or wriggle out. You are likely to tie yourself up into more and more embarrassing and eventually humiliating knots.

'I sometimes see your mother's ghost visiting first thing in the morning.'

My nephew did not seem surprised by my revelation.

We had time for a coffee; the station bar remained open.

'I insist,' my nephew said, as I reached into my pocket to buy the coffee. The little charmer had already bought dinner so it would have been only right to fork out my share for the evening. I had always been confused by money. In fact, once you start to moan on about it, you can talk about little else for far too long and be accused of boring those at your table, a bit like politics. Now I have little left, I curse the days I blew it on exotic holidays. Never be a slave to finance, my father used to drone, finger pointing, ensure money is your servant not your master. Oh fuck off! I know money makes the world go round, the world go round, the world go round and round and round and round and round and round . . . faster, faster, faster, faster, like a carousel at the fun fair running out of control. It will eventually disintegrate and crush even those spectators who did not have enough cash to take the ride, but were standing at the side waiting for a few coins to spill out.

My nephew smiled, shook his head, insisted, and ran his fingers through his damp hair, rain from his brown mane reflecting into the light, and then quite suddenly he reminded me of someone, his long hair, his fingers, his mouth. Older but it was him, it was D. I wanted to call out his name but I did not, instead I gazed into my nephew's brown eyes, lost in time.

'Come on, uncle!' My nephew was shaking me.

'Don't worry, just too much to drink, can't take as much these days.'

'Oxford, this is Oxford!' The stationmaster's words fell pompously from the speakers as the London train wheezed itself to a stop, spluttering over the joints.

'So my boy, send my best to your father, a fine man if ever

I've seen one.' How horribly simple it still was, and is, and presumably always will be, to tell a lie.

'Thank you, uncle,' he said, not believing a word and leant forward to give me a hug. A British Rail official interrupted our moment; 'Get on NOW, it's about to leave,' he ordered, and pointed a long nicotine-stained finger at the train.

I stood poker-faced and shooed him away. 'Shoooooo!' An excess of spittle flew into his face.

'Good journey, my boy!'

As the train disappeared from view, I left the platform with my shoulders slumped, but not before I walked up to the official, 'I'll have you know that I will not forgive you for that.'

He sneered back.

'What is the definition of disgusting?' I asked.

'I don't know. What is the definition of disgusting?" he answered instinctively.

'When great-granny or great-granddad kisses you good-night and puts the tongue in.'

*   *   *

When I woke there was no sign or scent of vomit, which was odd as I thought I had collapsed in a pool of it. I cannot go on – I understand that I have been saying this for the last twenty years but it is now true. The storm clouds were appearing over suburbia; my time was being called.

I sat up with a jolt. Something hit me on the leg. Shit! What was that? My dear landlady was throwing stones through the open window like local schoolchildren taking potshots at the village queer. I shuddered slightly and marched over to shout at her, 'Can't you knock on the fucking door like everyone else?' She smiled and asked whether I needed anything from the city centre. 'A set of razor blades,' I answered, 'to slit your throat.'

She let out a mock shriek and walked away from the house muttering oaths. She turned her head and chuckled with laughter. She was someone's daughter, someone's friend. The landlady, pregnant with pasta, took me in on my first day in Oxford. 'This way,' she had said, 'this is your new home,' and had heaved herself up one flight of stairs to show off my room, my new home full of dust, heavily worn carpets and a hundred stray cats. I am not an animal lover but if I had a choice, it would be the dog over the sentimental cat. And to reveal how nutty she was and is, she fluttered her eyelashes and fell in love with me.

The room is at its best in winter when the fire is lit and the logs are cackling. Chairs gathered round the warmth, feet on a tiger skin carpet, photo of Falston's 1st XI cricket team on the bookcase. It had become the place to visit, students knocking on my door to share a drink, to smoke my fags until I got bored and sent them away and everything evaporated except, for one ghostly figure all in white and always there.

The sun shone brightly although the dirty windows were doing their best to prevent any light from creeping through. The piles of scattered books on desk and floor created a sense of disorder, of slovenliness even. By the time the landlady had returned, I had had my bath and was ravenous. 'This is beginning to resemble a sty,' I moaned, 'clear it up would you?'

She came up with a vacuum cleaner and three cans of Special Brew. I really am too old to be drinking beer in the morning; the landlady wants me dead but will regret it when I fall to the ground clutching my chest.

'Roll me a cigarette, my dear?'

She took out her ever-present pouch of Golden Virginia, and rolled the tobacco quickly, so quickly in fact that if you didn't watch carefully it seemed you had witnessed a magic trick. She handed it over, even took the liberty of lighting it. What a strange creature she was; if I were totally honest she was my only friend. I did not like her but she was my only friend. Yet I treated her as a patient, a complicated specimen who carried her shoulders as if something momentous had happened early in her life, that she had never fully recovered and probably never would. Not having accepted this last fact she was unable to smile her way through all problems, depressions or even catastrophes. When, with most days, the past fades a little and time heals, she seemed oblivious to this. Her face was marked with lines, spots, and wrinkles like scratches on a record that had been over played. I once drunkenly conveyed my prognosis to which she let out a bellow of a laugh, 'You are talking about yourself, fool.'

*   *   *

I didn't usually go into the city centre. I preferred to remain in my manor of North Oxford, stretching from North Parade to Charlbury Road, either taking good walks or reading my collection of classic books. The modern trend is different. It now calls for fast fiction, full of fast action and characters. People want the instant fix. Instant art, immediate answers, short-term expediency, and even finding God without work. Few people have time to give the time of day these days. They forget that life is a marathon and not a sprint. They should remember that by running fast to the finish line, you tend to reach the end quickly. This was far from how I have lived my life. My pace has gradually grown slower and slower and I have had more time to pause and think about the whole range of my emotions and therefore feeling my pain more sharply. Perhaps that is where I am getting things wrong and not being able to fit in. The slow courtship is out and the fundamental ingredient of peace is pace.

Tonight was different. I had untied my shackles and rejoined the human race. I had been roped into attending a ghastly musical to raise cash for the Radcliffe Infirmary. A pretty doctor had treated me the previous week when, apparently, I had been discovered in my local pub lying with my head on the table in a pool of wine and a slither of sick. The doctor shook me heartily, 'Wake up, sir, this is no time for a sleep!' His diagnosis was that I had had too much to drink. I immediately regained my senses and denied his impertinent accusation.

'Don't talk such tosh,' but melted when I saw how attractive he was. He lost no time chatting me up and by closing time had sold me a ticket to the Playhouse.

'It will be a memorable evening,' he promised. I grinned knowing that he was lying though his teeth.

So here I was preparing for the evening. Time for a shave, I felt the coarseness of my growth. I did not want to be unshaven, not that night; best foot forward and all that! I set about squeezing the foam on to my face. My hair wet from the splash of water. Sometimes when I looked at myself, I found the sight so painful I had promised that all mirrors be removed, taken off the walls never to return. I shaved through the thick lather and cut myself, or at least thought I had cut myself but however hard I looked no blood emerged. I leant my head over the sink and splashed warm water over my face wiping away any trace of soap. I slapped a designer brand aftershave over my clean face. I did not have a cut after all, the face was perfectly set, and the sting of the aftershave had given my face a rejuvenation that only moments before a stranger would have predicted to be impossible. I had been transformed and looking at my watch I was in perfect time to walk to the theatre, share a quick drink in the bar, full of sexy doctors, and a glance at the programme; how bourgeois I was becoming.

'Where are you going?' the landlady asked.

'Out!'

'Quick drink before you go?'

I looked at my watch. 'Who the hell do you think I am?' I replied, if only to stop the head games, 'An alcoholic?'

*　　*　　*

I walked down Banbury Road towards St Giles, clenched fist, muttering something indistinguishable. A black saloon car slowed, the driver dressed in black tie. He eyed me suspiciously and then the car moved away slowly like a hearse. I didn't give it much thought at the time other than he must be going to the same event.

The street outside the Playhouse was crammed with middle aged women in long dresses and high heels escorted by men in dinner jackets; people half waving to each other. 'Tickets please.' My open shirt did not exactly create the right impression. It was still early so I went up to the bar.

'You look as if you need one,' said the impertinent barman in a rather too loud tone.

'I am not quite sure what you mean,' I said, 'but pour me a large gin.'

A plethora of highly pretentious conversation drowned the atmosphere. Oh, the exaggerated and loudness of the insecure! 'Some people say you can best judge a civilisation on how it treats its dead . . . depressing subject I suppose but death is well worth talking about,' preached a middle class woman with peculiar looks who told anyone who wanted to look closely enough that she had been in a collision with life. Her slightly dim friend laughed, not knowing what she meant, and I gave an enthusiastic echo. A polite conversation followed and the best thing that came out of it was a free glass of white wine. 'No I insist,' said the dim one as she opened her bag while I pretended to look for cash in my pocket. Yes, that old game. I had a few sips, continued my fixed smile and planned my escape but would you believe, a deep old feeling came surfacing to the fore, a feeling of good manners.

'Let me treat you both to another drink.'

'How very kind!' they answered in unison.

'That is generous of you, sir,' whispered the barman sarcastically as he poured the wine.

Insubordinate sod and thankfully the bell rang for the start of the performance before I had to lay out for them.

'Should I keep these for the interval?' He asked.

'Watch my lips . . . NO!' I said, and waved goodbye to the two ladies who had continued their prattle, repeating their gossip like a record that had missed a groove and got stuck, and I strode out of the bar.

'Programme?' An excited girl puffed and panted.

'I beg your pardon?'

'I was asking whether you wanted a programme, the money goes to the hospital.'

'Don't be so damn silly,' I replied, 'I have spent enough already!' She instinctively smiled and then seeing I was being serious backed away, as if I was carrying something that was contagious.

My ticket was at the end of the front row of the stalls; the seat next to mine was empty. At least I could rest my elbows on both arms without the ritual fight. The chatter from the audience faded and some latecomers found their places in the last second of light.

'Excuse me,' a young man walked by and fell to his seat. I immediately recognised him as the driver in the black saloon. His large forearm rested on the arm, his expensive watch sparkled briefly in the dark. Or was he lighting something, but no flame ensued. Help! It looked uncomfortably like the blade of a knife. The musical started and I edged away, convinced I was about to be stabbed. I thumped the top of my knee. I must stop drinking so much. I can't take it anymore. I had the shakes, held my hands together to give some balance – I needed a drink!

The play opened to a surge of activity, like a cluster of hens running madly around when just about to be fed. The audience remained unmoved, as if they had heard all the jokes before. The man to my side whom I realised was simply watching the performance, tutted; I presumed at the sheer lack of talent on view. He had a lime scent, a brown thick mane of hair falling just below his collar. His aftershave soothed my mind; I had smelt it before. The sound of his breathing through his perfectly formed nose was an exciting diversion from what was going on the stage. My nerves had calmed and now my neighbour's presence had begun to soothe my mind and my soul. I was tempted to ask the question, 'Do I know you?' but resisted. I resisted because I momentarily convinced myself that the question was not needed. I believed it to be D. D, twenty years on and as beautiful as always. I managed to remain calm, staying cool, hoping and praying that this was the moment, the moment that I had waited for, each minute, each day since we last met. I clasped my hands in self-restraint. What to do next? Again my mood started to shift. I felt like one of those great painters faced by a blank canvas: it was not the subject matter you remember so much as the way to deal with it. I went in search of honesty but only found a lack of it; my mind paced. I wanted to seize his hand and tell him I loved him but surely that would have been a definition of insanity; to repeat a crass action and expect a different result. I was becoming excited and frustrated; another uncomfortable mixture.

The play broke suddenly for its interval, the lights went on and the tone of the audience changed. I was so eager and desperate to get to the bar before anyone else that I surged through the stalls before remembering that I forgot to study more clearly my neighbour's face. I turned, praying he would be right behind. I turned so quickly that I stepped on my other foot and fell flat on my face, like in a cinema farce. A large man in a blue, sharply-cut suit and a striped tie which shouted military, asked if I was all right. His fit physique gave a feeling of inferiority. 'Of course I am all right!' and I pushed him away.

'Make it a brandy.' I placed my money directly into the barman's hand and took a long gulp. I turned to face the gathered, my stomach falling, my breathing heavy, gasping for air. How I hate making a spectacle of myself. I lit a cigarette, took a deep drag, and blew out the smoke. Had I really seen D? Had I, because of my desperation, my addiction for drink, missed telling him that I thought of his face every day? I stood and swept my fingers through my hair. Maybe it was what I deserved, a fleeting tantalising moment. And then I started to convince myself that there was every good reason he would return for the second half.

'Barman, barman, another drink.'

'Can I have a light?' I turned and automatically struck a match. 'Thank you' came a voice not unlike a cello, smooth and deceiving, a voice I had not heard before. My own hands suddenly seemed small and weak.

For an instant we were standing together. Look at those eyes, so dark even in the dark, as the lights flash twice to signal the recommencement of the play . . . on and off, on/off like lightning. He turned and left without a thank you. Though our meeting was short it affected every sense: eye, ears and smell. Startled, I grabbed at the bar. Oh God, I was going to fall again! I became unsettled, startled from the precipitous encounter as when there is a sudden crash of cymbals in a gentle passage of music and you nearly jump from the seat. The noise increased. The hasteful babble of one hundred and one half-conversations as the audience returned to the auditorium. I staggered away and into the bathroom. I needed to take timeout . . . out . . . out . . . ouuuuuuuuuuuuuuuuuuuuuu uuuuuuuuuut. Otherwise one covers the situation with the pus of pondering about how it should have been dealt with differently. I should have grabbed him by the lapels and held him against the wall, screamed my question that had suffocated me over the years. 'Why did you tell the headmaster?' I looked at the sweat covering my hands and realised that my head was aching, my heart was pounding, sex glands swelling.

A man was looking in the mirror adjusting his black tie. The bell had rung again.

'We better hurry up!' he said.

My wet hand acted on its own by fashioning itself into the shape of a gun, my lips made a little explosion and my mouth stretched itself into a wide smile. He starred back, I sneered in return and without another word he paced out of view. I splashed water over my face, paused and followed high-heeled ladies nonchalantly walking back into the theatre as if it was their right. I looked round, where was he? The seat next to mine remained empty. Perhaps he found the first half so dire that he could not face the second?

The music struck up, the orchestra sounding like the tune the cat died of. It couldn't have been this bad but all memory of what I had seen previously had vanished. I wrenched quite deliberately during a surge from the orchestra, head down, lowered. Had the barman slipped a 'Mickey Finn' into my drink? I was feeling as awful as I had for a long time and that was saying something. How to get out without falling, without being noticed? I sat through the second act believing that my D had in fact moved and was directly behind, eyes daggered into the back of my head piercing my shoulders. I turned round quickly, head jerking. I felt I would find him again instinctively amongst the crowd. I was ready, prepared to turn, as a fight ensued on the stage, the orchestra was groaning, raising its tempo. I turned and my eyes connected to five rows behind towards the centre of the row. And there he was, staring right back at me. His eyes of teak stabbing, unmoving and full of recognition; he nodded his head, rebuked my self-pity. He licked his lips. I can hear him now, tutting and muttering. 'Coles,' he mouthed. I could hear my name being shouted loud into my ears. 'COLES . . . COLES . . . COLES' My imagination filled in what the eye only glimpsed, like being on a moving train, staring out of the window and for a moment catching a scene and filling in the story.

I leant forward like a diamond valuer and in one swift movement I turned again to find D's chair empty. He had gone. He had disappeared. Where did he go? I felt panic, a sharp unease; I left my seat and crept up the aisle as a song started up on stage. A hand grabbed out at my arm. I was startled and glanced at someone sitting at the end of a row. It was the doctor who had seduced me into buying a ticket. He mouthed something inaudible. He reminded me of someone who, for once in his life, had been the first to fill his bingo card but for some reason was unable to call out. So I answered the question that he was trying to ask.

'No it has been the most awful of evenings full of turgid music combined with talentless performances. Thank you for nothing.' I smiled and made my way out onto the street, catching my breath and then vomiting into the gutter on a humid summer evening with dark sky hanging uneasily above. A procession of cars drove slowly along Beaumont Street. It was as if I had been slapped on my face and everything I thought I had remembered reverberated, like being kicked in the ribs.

I walked slowly and uneasily back onto the Banbury Road in the breathless sinking night. I kept looking back as if I were being followed: there was no one. A strip of vomit lay on my shirt. I walked with pace and when I passed anyone, I veered on to the edge of the road to avoid contact with their eyes. I popped into the off-license and went straight to the fridge and grabbed a can of Special Brew. I paid with the exact amount.

'Thank you, sir,' meowed the shop assistant.

Ugrgh that word 'sir'. I have been called it half my life but when someone calls me 'sir' on first meeting it riles my very being. Some may be flattered but I for one, consider the person an anachronistic creep who is trying to ingratiate themselves in the most charmless way or simply taking the piss, as when calling a humble constable 'officer'.

The can was drunk by the drunk before reaching home; it numbed the pain.

I collapsed, stretched out on the bed. Thank God I had opened the window before I left for the theatre. A hint of wind crept through the side of the curtain. God it was hot.

Knock, knock . . .

Oh God who is there . . . ?

'Clifford?'

Damn she had heard me.

'Hello.'

I walked to the door without opening.

'What do you want?'

'I found a money clip with your credit card.'

I opened the door and standing in front of me was my landlady in knickers and bra, holding my Visa card.

'It is yours, Clifford, it has your name on it . . . here, look, Clifford Coles.'

At first I didn't recognise my name; I snatched it and sneered.

'Is everything all right, Clifford?' she asked, as if talking in code.

'Everything is fine.' I wiped a drip of sweat from my brow, flicked it towards her and slammed the door.

'I have a fine bottle of brandy for you, Clifford.'

'Fuck off!'

Soon she was yelling from outside at my window, 'You bastard!'

I am old enough to know the difference between someone who is genuinely angry and when he or she is not. Her groans were the last thing I needed. I was becoming so disillusioned. I no longer trusted my judgment or in fact my state of mind.

I crawled into bed this time with clothes thrown to the floor. Must get the landlady to wash those stains; she had seen much worse. I thumped my pillow and myself to sleep.

*   *   *

Ladies and gentlemen, and especially youngsters, I shall be brief as I am sure you have something more important to do. This morning I had a spotlight of clarity – groan, groan counterbalanced by a few hear, hears – please be quiet in the back. Yes, clarity. When I woke this morning and saw the sick over my clothes, brown brogues thrown from one corner to the other, empty bottles dropped where ever I had drunk the last drop and an ashtray full of butts, I realised that I would not die of alcohol. I readily admit that may surprise many of you and I have had many excellent doctors warning with a voice slipping into a sense of urgency, that drink would be the death of me. But it is not to be, for although I know my body is collapsing and my mind has begun to take its last leap before meeting its maker, it will not be the drink that drags me from this life but madness. For delusion has begun in earnest. I am learning life's cost that once one is properly paranoid, one can be paranoid about everything and anything. The slightest gesture on someone else's part being intended for oneself, a particular tune being played for one's benefit, all conversation and gestures becoming part of a worldwide conspiracy and the mind is bugged. One is at the very black centre of existence, the evil part of human nature that is in all of us and should not be allowed to . . .

This fast becoming rather interesting last sentence was cut short by a heavy bang on the door. A black cup of coffee was placed on my desk. 'Can't you fucking knock?' The landlady was about to ignore my tirade and then before leaving gave a mock Nazi salute. Charming!

'I am going away for the night, so you will have to call upon another slave.'

'Just one moment, dear landlady,' I replied. 'Before you piss off, go fetch me another bottle.'

'I'll go and fetch a bottle as long as you promise that once you finish it, you will break it into a thousand pieces and stab the glass into your head.'

I was in no mood for necromancy so I kept quiet.

*   *   *

I finished my crossword, and walked to the pub.

'Having a good day?' the insincere barman asked.

I said nothing, instead listened to the clouds rumbling, somewhere near somewhere far. 'What the hell was that?'

'The weather is breaking.' A moustached stranger replied from a seat by the window. A mad old woman shrieked, 'It is the end of the world.' The pub was full of its regulars, my nightly companions: Charlie from the Laundromat, his mouth opened wide and long and you needn't have heard the words to understand the story; Dr Tim, the Oxford don, a small man in his sixties, giving quick sideward glances that told a hundred untold stories and carpenter Phil – when is a door not a door?

When it is made by Phil.

'Jesus, pour another drink!'

The barman held the glass to the light to check on any dirt and poured a large whiskey. 'Your usual,' he said.

It is fine to call it my usual when I have been frequenting the pub for over twenty years but disturbing when it is announced on a second visit and I scolded him for doing so at the time.

'Don't be impertinent,' I remember saying and ever since he has repeated his turn; I enjoyed his spirit though. Not many have dared to answer back.

The 'moustache' asked for my name.

'Coles,' I replied.

'We minorities must stick together, Mr Coles.' He looked Jewish, very Jewish, lit a foreign cigarette and handed it to me, his hands massive and hairy. The cigarette took effect, the deep thick weight of French tobacco burning my lungs, brain barbed wire.

'I've been called many things, but never a Jew.'

'I never thought you were. It is not what I meant.' He preened his moustache, paused and said, 'Please sit with me.'

'Thank you,' I said, trying to be the nice person.

We looked around for a suitable table away from those ears pierced with antennas. He proposed a toast from his expensive bottle of red wine, 'To all the beautiful spoiled people in this world.' I smiled back at my handsome companion and the day, although now early evening, started to feel better. In fact, it felt absolutely delicious.

Strange how the appreciation in one's life can depend on one's mood. Moustaches had always been particularly revolting in my eyes but because he made a fine toast and had the finest of features I felt positively good; his moustache looked delightful.

Help yourself to a drink sweetheart; put your feet up and I will put on a little floor show for you! The barman chucked new ice into a fresh glass and poured my usual. Before my new friend could get a word in, I was putting the world to rights.

'It is all right for you,' I said pointedly at my companion, 'you being a pretty young bastard. For the likes of me, the more I feel age encroaching, the more I tend to react to it, paradoxically revealing it all the more obviously even to a disinterested spectator. If you are the only one wearing a mask or fancy dress you tend to get noticed.'

The stranger did not offer a lifeline, but simply asked, 'And how long have you been wearing a costume?'

'Ever since I turned ugly,' I snorted.

Another round? It was my turn and soon I was placing a bottle in the centre of the table. 'Not quite the same but a close relative.'

'Have you written a book?' he asked. He must have been reading my churned mind as I had only that afternoon thought about starting a new novel.

'I might have.' I teased.

'About your life?'

'I have finished a novel on unrequited love. Absolute drivel of course and will never let it be published. You know the sort you simply can't put down. Sort of stuff you buy in the airport, even bump in to the author in a huff because there are not enough of the books on display. I call it a novel but it is not a novel at all . . . ' and then I noticed he had switched off and I did not complete my sentence. Fuck, the last thing I wanted to be considered was a bore but I recognised that my unsociable life might well have been pointing me in that direction.

'Have you experienced unrequited love?' he asked.

'Haven't we all!'

'Have we?' He asked as if he knew something I did not. 'Haven't you ever been satisfied with your life, Mr Coles?'

'Full of questions aren't we?'

I can be driving a cart down one side of a track and be sure that the other side is less full of potholes and ruts; so across I

164

go. But no! It is just as rough, even rougher: so back I go, to my former reality. Also after screwing my ass off in a by-the-hour hotel, I go for a piss, and see through another door a perfection that you instinctively know has been a better fuck than your own lover, so that out of your near memorable experience the creature that later haunts you is the one you did not have. And here, at last in the midst of an action-filled, potentially riveting, scene, I wish to whatever God that I were somewhere, in fact, anywhere, else.

The bell rang for last orders. I felt a slight dizziness come over me. I felt as nervous as a man who was very tired but could not sleep. The stranger had asked me to join him on a walk. I had drunkenly agreed. I had let myself into something that was beyond my control, the drink had gone to my head unlike ever before, well, unlike any time I could remember. The face from the theatre flashed subliminally in my mind. The thought of the previous night seemed to make me more drunk than I could remember.

As I walked outside, the weather was sultry and I started to gulp the night's air.

'Do you have hiccups?' Moustache joked.

'I do but it think it would be more polite to simply ignore them,' I replied.

'Someone better give you a fright!' he said.

'Oh no, I have already had my fright for today, thank you. It came in the shape of a tall figure smoking foreign cigarettes and asking people they have just met to go for a walk.'

He stopped, let out a deep sigh and suggested we go to 'my place' for a drink.

By the time we reached my house, I had already begun to wish the Moustache had kept his prying nose out of it.

The path leading to the front of the house was thin gravel with loose stones plunging into the soul of the foot. The front door was stripped of blue paint with number twenty-four scrawled on as if by a graffiti artist. As I opened the door three cats skipped past our feet into the dark of the night.

'This way,' I beckoned my Jewish stranger to follow. The hallway was dark, an underlying whiff of cat. I grabbed the banister in need of support; it was that dark. The light in the hallway was not working, the bulb had burst and we trod on broken glass. I thought I had mistakenly grabbed something huge and hairy, perhaps the Jew's hand, and jumped to my side losing whatever cool I had left to lose. It was in fact another cat that, because of fright, jumped over my head and scrambled away.

* * *

I grabbed for the nearest bottle; it was a liver-bashing, mind-boggling slug of a drink. I then poured my guest one.

'What do we have here?' He had picked up Falston's First XI photo. 'And who is this?' he asked, simpering like that furtive figure seen in the red light district picking up pornographic magazines. 'I asked who this is?' He said, pointing at D's head, the grease of his finger rubbing on to the glass. His immorality repulsed me, his face swollen into a boil ready to be burst, his blood exploding to every corner of the room.

'STOP THAT!' I yelled like a bawling infant. I felt I was drowning, watching helplessly as the water rose to my chest and up to my throat.

I snatched the photograph to my chest – a very feminine hissy fit. 'Leave that alone!' I stood clasping at my prize possession mourning the fact I was no longer there, mourning that I was no longer teaching and guiding the young that would one day lead our country. I cursed the waste of it all. Damn, damn, damn!

I turned to see the stranger silhouetted against the street glow and although I found him handsome and I had a bell of a beautiful thought, I felt a heave in my stomach; his presence suffocating. I clicked my fingers hoping he would disappear. Clickety-click but he just stood smiling, describing me as a 'bad tempered old bugger.' He offered another cigarette. He waved it in front of me.

'Do you want it?' He teased with a hint of a grin on the face pulling the cigarette away. So that's your game. 'Don't tease those more intelligent than you, it never works,' I sneered.

'You're not particularly intelligent Coles. You're the fool because unlike me you can't admit who or what you are. You have spent too long disappearing unto your own head, creating your story and it is not that of reality.'

'Is that your final analysis?' I asked. Judge not and ye shall not be judged. I watched his heart bleed as a phalanx of jackbooted Conservatives goose-stepped in, splintering his blood and soul into the darkness and then being dragging him away to an over the horizon place called Hell.

He approached, jabbing his finger. I suddenly realised that I could not move. I tried to put one foot in front of the other but it was impossible.

'If I prayed, I would pray for you. You and I are the same Coles, the difference is I admit it, you do not.' I once more tried to move but still I couldn't. The more I pushed forward, the more I pulled back. I felt desperate like a lunatic that escaped the asylum but had been caught by men in white coats trying to get a straight jacket around, screaming at me until they suddenly let go and I spring forward.

'I recognised you as soon as you walked in to the pub. We have been touched by the same curse,' the moustache said.

Had I turned into someone so obvious, that my mere presence gave the game away? I remembered at Falston how the perverts in our midst were as transparent as cling film. Had I turned into someone so obvious, that my mere presence gave the game away?

On my desk a penholder was full of cutlery. There was a bread knife calling my name. 'Take me!' it said. 'I will tear the bastard to pieces.' I had a shiver of portent. From the street, there was a distracting yell, a howl as if someone was being castrated. I had heard it many times before. I let out a deep sigh. I went to the window and there was the landlady. She was sitting in the middle of the road. She reminded me of a child who had her television confiscated because of overuse, and now crouched in her usual place staring at the empty corner.

Feeling that she was being watched, she turned her head and chuckled. She started to pick herself up slowly as if she had lead on her back. Straightening her legs, she fell back onto the street. I went out to help; although I hated her, I also pitied her. She pulled me down to eye level, trying to jerk her knee into my groin.

'Fuck you!' she groaned. She smelt of dead meat, the stench making me giddy. She grabbed hold of my scrotum.

'Try to stand up,' I said, 'we have an audience,' and pointed to my room. The landlady grabbed my arm and pulled herself up. 'I am going to make an official complaint about you,' she said walking in a zig-zag line, tears streaming down her face.

God did I ever get this drunk?

'Make that complaint,' I yelled after her, the blood rushing to my head.

I looked up again and Moustache was still looking out of the window smoking, the smell of his cigarette splintering the still night. When I reached my room, I was greeted by his smile, as wide as his shoulders. I had caught a reflection of myself in the mirror and did not recognise the face but then the more I looked, the more I loathed. I had worn a mask and had become oddly attached, figuratively and literally. I was loathe to take it off. What if I had grown suddenly horribly hirsute, hooked nose, thin lipped?

I needed a long kiss of life. He did not actively encourage what I would call embrace but acquiesced by not flexing a muscle, and then my breath was taken away, for he no longer wore a moustache but carried a hairless body with the darkest of eyes, and the gentlest of breath. My conscience rumbled, sometimes clapping. We kissed, and I knew that it was not who or how we are that matters, but how we deal with the whoever and however we are, for as I held this body in my arms, I knew that D was by my side once again, now grown and indeed a man. I had finally met him as an equal. 'D,' I whispered and I hung onto his shoulders like a solitary glove draped over a fence in the unlikely hope of its owner returning to retrieve it.

I pulled away and leant against the fireplace to regain my balance when suddenly I felt as if I had been struck with force on the back of the head. And my mind went back to another time when my body felt warm, even glowed on a hot summer's afternoon. The school field was swarming with boys competing in an athletic meet. D had just won the long jump competition and had broken the school record. In celebration, he had taken his shirt off. His face lit up and he ran towards me revelling like an animal that had just had his first kill. I could not hold back my longing, not sure if these were thoughts that distinguished man from beast. When he finally reached me, wide-eyed and out of breath, he shrieked triumphantly, 'I won, sir, I won.' He gave me a beautiful smile.

I smiled back, not dissimilar to a hundred previous smiles but this time with love.

I took a deeper look through the eyes; you have the most beautiful eyes, beneath the mouth, under the tan. I felt so happy and so desperate and died a little. I turned my head away to hide my tiptoeing tears. From the sea air, from sorrow, from pure joy? Most likely a mix of all three.

'I am proud of you, so proud.'

'Thank you, sir. Thannnnk you.' And with that, he ran away under the sun that suddenly turned red, hanging there for a few long last minute, for a week, for a year.

He was eleven years old.

*   *   *

'Feeling better?' the landlady asked.

I was undressed except for my boxer shorts, and lying in bed propped up by three pillows.

'Drink this,' and she passed a glass of aspirin, the trace of foam still bubbling on top. The room had been tidied, books neatly piled, glasses cleared, unwashed mugs nowhere to be seen. The only remnant from the night before was the smell of cigarettes giving the room the scent of a French café. How I yearned for a coffee, how I yearned for an explanation. But first things first and I sent off the landlady to get me some breakfast. I was not sure of the time but the sun was bright and had the morning feel. It was not long before the landlady reappeared with a cup of coffee. I thanked her and drank in silence. Fuck! It was bitter, probably poisoned. No sugar! I looked to the fireplace and saw the Falston photograph placed at the exact spot it had always been – it was the first point my eyes met in the morning.

'Where is the stranger?'

She shrugged her shoulders.

'The dark moustached man I was with last night'

'I saw no one . . . ' She replied with a certain tone to her voice that reopened a crack that I managed to paper over. Once I had collapsed, he must have made a quick exit.

I had no energy to deal with her; I felt like someone faced with a full plate of pasta and with no appetite. The stranger I presumed had pissed off and who could blame him? The landlady had laid out fresh clothes; last night's were soiled and she said with a sinister edge, 'I am having them cleaned.'

*   *   *

I decided to visit a doctor. I had had enough of the headaches, guttural coughs, and blood-stained phlegm in the morning. I sensed the end was nigh and yesterday's blackout was enough to check my health. If I was dying, I wanted to know how long I had left.

The doctor's surgery door opened smartly. A smallish man rushed past pale-faced, clearly just heard some bloody awful news. The nurse asked me to wait in the waiting room.

'He won't be a minute. Have a look at the lousy magazines.' I started to have second thoughts. Why was I doing this? Was this from a final surge of responsibility? Or from a crazed feeling that I had more to offer the world? Perhaps I am just getting old or older and older? Suffering from cancer? Smoking too much after failing again to give up; now puffing endlessly on one after another. Senility? Thinking a fly is a wasp. Drooling or even foaming at the mouth. Reading the menu with one eye, indulging in nostalgia, bumping into anything and everything . . .

'The doctor will see you now, Mr Coles.'

He listened to my heart – tut-tut; he nodded, picked and pushed. He was giving me the full examination, lifting the eyelids, pressing the chest, turning over my body, and pushing a stethoscope into my back.

'Take deep breaths, now slow shallow breaths, even and steady . . . even and . . . ' He did all this so meticulously yet with such a lack of compassion. He let out a giant sigh, walked to his desk, scribbled something down on foolscap lined paper and returned for another prod. 'You have never really looked after yourself, have you?'

171

'I have been having blackouts, morning headaches . . . worse than ever before.'

'Perhaps it is psychosomatic,' he said, not believing his own words.

'Are you depressed?' The doctor asked.

'Ever since I was ten.'

'Do you want to tell me something – expose your sinful secrets?'

'Yes, doctor, I am a homosexual.'

'I gathered that!' he replied, not missing a beat.

The doctor turned into a priest in front of my very eyes; pale hands, lucent face, heavy breathing that wouldn't stop, believing he had been sent by God to heal the sick.

'What scares you?' he asked.

'Hell,' it was my turn, not miss a beat. Hell, where we see our sins as closely as a doctor inspecting the retina of our eyes. Hell is where they say to you, this is where you went wrong and bit by bit our mistakes are held to the light. You should never have treated those boys in such a manner; you should have been more sensitive to those souls who searched for your help. And the more you cry out in defence, the more retribution you are served. Bit by bit exposed in the light.

'And your wish?'

'To be accepted in Heaven . . . to have a chance of resurrection. Simply Heaven is not Hell.'

I heard a 'tut-tut'; not the reaction I expected from my doctor. He wrote down someone's name.

'I will call the John Radcliffe Hospital and ask whether they would fit you in within the next hour.'

Shit, it must be grave.

*   *   *

172

I had my test and was asked to return to meet the specialist twenty-four hours later. I had mentioned his name to Professor Tim and he knew him well, 'He is writing a doctoral thesis which, alas, he has never quite completed! He seems to be one of those that will forever do the rounds . . . '

The specialist looked up and stared into my eyes. His elbows were on the armrests of his chair. So this is what an execution feels like. He turned and popped something into his mouth. It smelt like peppermint. Can I have one? He passed a Polo from his own hand and beckoned me towards him as if about to tell a secret.

'Only out of wreckage can a new life emerge,' he mumbled.

What was he suggesting? I was going to have to suffer still further to sink before I could survive? To reach my individual rock bottom before I could truly live! The results had poured in. His prognosis boomed out like an express train exploding through the station or the gambler listening to the racing on the radio when the car goes under a bridge and the transmission fades. What did he say? Please repeat Professor? Again he tried, but this time it felt like the exact moment the funnel and smokestack screeeeams!

' . . . if you don't look after yourself you will be dead very soon. It seems life's questions have taken their toll.'

I thought that is what he said. As he wrote out a long, long prescription, he muttered words like 'stroke', 'relapse', 'serious', 'regular checks'. He then gave me a brief 'thumbs up' which I presumed to mean, 'All will be well'. But whatever, it would go down as the most subliminal sign of 'You are going to make it' ever recorded.

I admit that when I left the specialist's office, I became overcome with sentimentality and in the middle of St Giles hid my face in my sleeve and wept for I recognised that I was a weak man. 'Must not weep,' I urged myself, 'you have nothing to weep for,' but in fact I wept for my loneliness. There can be nothing lonelier than when you leave a doctor's office and have no one to turn to.

I sat gloomily in Browns Café in the covered market and acknowledged the reality that doubt, fear, hate, probably all negative feeling, results in life's sickness. I tried to look proud to anyone looking in my direction but in truth, I was still fighting back the tears. There had been a realisation that I had been sick for a long time and that I had lost everything I ever wanted. Is pain growth? I asked myself. I knew I was dressed like death, slouching, grey-haired, grey-skinned, grim-faced and believed that I was passing that dividing line from eccentricity into madness.

*   *   *

I woke early at five in the morning, feeling dreadful, as if with a steel band round my head. In fact, I did not as much wake up as sit up. What! Yet another hangover? Was it the aftershock of yesterday's warning for my health or the bottle of Polish vodka that lay empty beside my bed? Yet I hadn't drunk that much, had I? Just a few swigs of what was admittedly potent stuff. I might do well to remember the old adage: 'It isn't how much you drink that matters, but what it does to you.' To stop drinking is easy; it's staying stopped that can be hard.

I felt cheated, as if I now had that morning after feeling, when I had done fuck-all the night before, which, come to think of it, I had; done fuck-all, I mean. So with my pounding head, hot heart, sick soul and some unremembered but nasty nightmare, I decided to walk, get some good decent English fresh air, good clean thoughts, and rid my mind of torture.

The sun was getting warmer. The hangover was drifting and the early risers had already had their breakfast and smoked their first fag of the day. In fact, I decided from that morning I

174

would be more polite to everyone, everything, even to hangovers. By making that quiet vow, I began to feel much better and was finally learning that there was no need for hangovers at all: simply don't drink so much or simply don't drink at all. Never too late to learn!

I set off by foot to the River Cherwell, close to the boathouse. I found a space that was relatively empty except for a willing few, keen to catch the first rays of the morning sun. Lying not far from where I had pitched my book, towel, and bathrobe was a man, Swedish was my instinctive guess. Even from some distance I could not fail to notice that what I could see of his flesh was very white and hairless, not unlike my sickly sight. He was reading a book. I watched him for several minutes, and not once did he raise his eyes from the page. I felt a similar sensation to spotting someone on TV who never blinks! In fact, the Swede concentrated so hard that it struck me that he might have been feigning, like a snob commuter apparently reading a broadsheet newspaper but with a cheap tabloid hidden inside.

There was a small cabin for those with a certain amount of modesty to change in. I had decided for the first time, or shall we say, 'For the first time in years,' to go for a swim. I put down my book, ran to the cabin, and changed into my long swimming trunks bought many years ago. I came back to the Cherwell pulled off my towel and took two confident strides over to the river leaving the towel at the very edge. 'SWIM WITH CARE, NO SPLASHING' a wooden board announced.

'Jump straight in, jump straight in,' I repeated quietly to myself, clench-fisted, knowing from past experience, although a long time ago, that it is ultimately better not to dabble a big toe in order to test the temperature of the water, and definitely not to take the slow groin numbing, scrotum searing, descent.

I tightened my weak resolve but I hesitated. There was no

175

one else on the verge of entering the river whose body language or facial expressions I could analyse, before I hit the water, in order to deduce whether it was, as I half suspected, fucking freezing, nor some kind person who could assure me either that, 'it is really warm', a kind white lie or give the truth and nothing but . . . that: 'Yes, it's bloody freezing when you first get in, but bloody great when you get used to it.'

'You will love it,' called out the emaciated Swede who had clearly been watching my hesitant steps.

That was all I needed, a metaphorical push, so I jumped.

UGH!! UUUGH!!! It was like plunging from tropical heat into snow! I felt the heart gasp, and briefly ask itself whether this was a good time for it to stop for good. Yes, for me that would end a number of complications, a massive coronary personally given by the River Cherwell would be a romantic end to any writer/teacher. But then I remembered that the best seller remained stored in the mid-drift of my mind. Once I had emerged out of the shock, I began to feel good and could readily have gone through it all again. Where is that dividing line between pain that is sheer pain, and pain that is pleasure? Dripping candle wax on flesh, or being smacked firmly on the ass when you fail your school test. I always believed the boys enjoyed the sensation and moaned with satisfaction. It was something I had adopted in my Falston days. A heavy wallop if the boy failed to give a right answer, but for me the excitement was too much and had to be curtailed, in case one of the boys saw my groin and asked that old adage, 'Is that a gun in your pocket Mr Coles or are you just pleased to see me?'

The Swede jumped in without hesitation in a 'hey look at me' sort of way and looked deeply unattractive in the process. He immediately swam over. His fingers fell towards my body but as soon as he had brushed my skin, a shock of guilt went through him as powerful as any snap of a shark. He pulled back his hand abruptly and looked to see if anyone had noticed. There was no one in sight; he needn't have worried.

'You should be more careful,' I hissed and then put my finger to my lips. I moved forward and he started to retreat, 'Where are you going?' I asked. He did not answer. 'I am coming to get you,' I teased, and moved towards him, like a submarine emerging from the depths of the ocean. He looked nervous, consistently eyeing the bank to see if anyone was there. How odd we can all be at times? Only seconds before he was making an uncalled advance, and now that I was making the move, he was retreating.

'What turns you on?' I asked.

'I am sorry?'

'What turns you on?'

'What are you saying?' the Swede replied.

'What turns you on?' The needle in my head was stuck in a groove. I fell on to my back and started to splash ever so lightly like a child playing in its bath. Silence followed and then the Swede asked what I did for a living. A dreary question but I answered, 'I am a teacher.'

'No teacher gave me advice except in maxims of the sort: masturbation stunts growth or masturbation turns you blind. So that's your game, Mister?'

'I recently visited my old school and now I laugh at how diminutive the buildings are when only a few years before they were so foreboding and grim.'

I listened contently to the critique of his life until he said something like, 'I bet you were the type of teacher that would not be able to pass the exam whose syllabus you were supposedly teaching!'

I suddenly became very cold and threw a mini tantrum: Me, me, me, me. The great I or the Royal We. Mind your own fucking business. Male bitch that comes over uninvited and

177

takes it upon himself to criticise. You can criticise anything but not my ability to teach. You have no idea how gifted I am, how my boys benefit from my considered words.

'Don't come over and start to jeer at me, you offensive, dull Dane or whatever the fuck you are?'

'Keep your voice down,' was all he could say. There was a silence. A long silence. I had had enough.

'Thank you,' I said and trampled through the cold water to fetch my towel.

*   *   *

Lunch at the Cherwell Boathouse was the perfect antidote to the uninvited intrusion. I got dressed and felt famished. I always took this to be a good sign, a sign of good health; how wrong I must have been.

The restaurant was surprisingly sparse for late August. Sitting at the next table was a long-haired skinny person. I guessed he was male because I thought I could discern the fringes of a beard, although I had recently read an article in the *Oxford Mail* about females who cultivate facial hair. In my lifetime I had met a few old hags with moustaches. There was one on a short trip to Cumnor whom, when I turned down her advances, threatened to chop off her facial hair and send it to me in a matchbox.

Anyway whoever he or she was, it was wearing headphones and beating with its fingers on the side of the table. It was generally uncoordinated and I wanted to tap it on the shoulder and ask it to 'STOP!' But I was changing, becoming more tolerant of others, although I had a slight hiccup with that Swede that very morning. My instinct was to leave it alone and not make it jump out of its skin, for maybe it had a weakened heart and would collapse and die. So I remained hushed and whispered my order to the waiter, like someone quiet at another's prayers. It could not hear me: 'What do you call a person with headphones?'

'I don't know. What do you call a person with headphones?'

'Anything you like because he or she can't hear you!'

I looked out onto the river and tried to find some real peace, a rare selfish pleasure, refreshment for my rotting soul. I wanted to stop dredging the depths of my mind and instead concentrate on routine, preferably superficial. That vow lasted the time it took to prepare my chicken salad and of course I ended up thinking even more. I did not want to see death as some clinically established collapse of the brain or as transformation from animal into vegetable.

Who said, 'Never say die until the bones are rotting?'

*   *   *

After lunch and paying the overpriced bill, I remained seated and closed my eyes. The patterns began to roll, of black and white fireworks, and a dozen tiny carousels. Was I asleep? No, or giving my eyes a rest! Sweat and oil trickled down the forehead and through the lashes, and stung and finally drowned the fantasies, the fair, the fornication, the fornication in the fair, fair fantasies in the fornication . . .

I was awoken from my semi-siesta by a commotion coming from the cabin that I had changed in only a couple of hours before. It was a blood-curdling scream. It made me leap out of my skin.

A crowd had gathered and was mesmerised with something floating in the river.

'Make way, let me see,' I ordered the onlookers like a detective first on the scene. I thought it was a deluge of paraphernalia fallen from the riverbank, but it wasn't, it was indistinguishably a body. I felt nothing even when I saw its face; the face of the hairless Swede. The book he was reading

179

remained opened by his towel a few feet away.

I edged away and picked it up. He was reaching its finish, had ten pages to go. Poor sod would never know its ending. How extraordinary life is. Death seemed to be shadowing my mind, my physical being, but also the shape of the day.

The police arrived with excitement plastered over their faces; it was not every day there was a death on the River Cherwell. Again who said, 'There is nothing like death to get your mind going.'

'Looks like murder,' the younger of the two policemen said after the body was pulled out onto the bank. There was a dark mark smeared around his neck like a heavily drawn red felt pen.

'Take your time son, nine times out of ten an immediate prognosis is way off,' the senior officer tutted.

The Swede was dressed in pale yellow trunks and a blue shirt with a grey vest underneath. His body had folded like a swatted wasp and from my amateurish calculation must have been in the water for less than two hours. I looked at his face and judging from his expression there were only sweet memories. The body had begun to inflate due to drowning in river water. Salt water had the opposite effect. I had only read about this a week before; another of life's coincidences.

His clothes clung to his body weeping next to his pale skin.

'Who found the body?' asked the younger policeman, keen to regain points from his 'teacher'.

No one came forward. Don't they say that in a murder there is a fifty-fifty chance that the person who finds the body did the deed – 'he who smelt it, dealt it?' Had the Swede's death been a tragic mistake, like a shot fired by someone so innocent that he is unaware of such things as safety catches? Even of which way to point the gun! Or was he like a school child that tied his hands to a railroad track with no intention of killing himself, only to scream out when the loop of the rope is grabbed by the locomotive and he is dragged under? I think not. Come to think of it, how could anyone know that he did not intend to kill himself? The presumption, judging the dire hopelessness of the action, is deplorable; I scolded myself for such a thought.

It was time to move on, enough of this gaping nonsense. Have a look, yes, but then move on. How I loathe those cars backing up traffic after an accident just so they catch a better view. I looked once more at the face and seemed to scowl. I was unsure whether it was disapproving, or warning or simply telling me to get a bloody move on? There was no time to delve any further. I blew the Swede a kiss, whispered a 'see you soon,' and returned home under the dying sun.

*   *   *

Carrying a genuine smile on my face, I set off for my nightly visit to the Rose and Crown. I dressed quickly, not before giving my body a good quick rub down. I felt thirty years younger, peak condition. How seeing the Swede lying dead on the riverbank had me feeling so much better. To repeat a quote from my doctor 'quintessentialises' my day, my life: 'Only out of wreckage can new life emerge.'

I was poured my usual and instead of taking a quick slug from my first drink of the night, I sat down with it and befriended each sip, one of which was toasted to the dead Swede, in quite a sentimental fashion. I crossed myself and thought how much more comfortable it would be to die in the dark than on a bright summer's afternoon in full view of strangers. I crossed myself again and in an indefinable moment my calm turned into sobs. Sobs for the Swede: 'Through the voyage of my tears I sail to the dead.'

And then the universe played yet another card and I knew that old adage that 'everything has its reason' was true.

'Mr Coles?'

I looked up. My mind first sped to, 'I have no idea who this is.' He was a tall unsmiling chap, handsome though.

'Mr Coles, do you remember me?'

I had heard the secret to all happiness was a bad memory, clearly not for me. And now as I write this from the memory of when the contents of a bottle fit to just below the rim of a glass, I looked into his light eyes and recalled where we had met before.

'You were at Falston?'

'Yes, sir, I was on your cricket team.'

The two blue-stocking chinless girls who he had left behind at a neighbouring table threw disapproving looks. What do they see? Maybe they were told some gossip. 'Look there is my ex-teacher, the old pervert Mr Coles.'

'Buy yourself a drink and make mine a double.' He turned down my offer of money – fool! – and went to the bar that had all of sudden filled with an intake of German tourists. The landlord was fast losing his cool. He was showing favouritism to anyone who waved eye-catching bank notes in the air, hinting in the manner of the waving, that any change would be for him to keep if only he served them a fucking drink. In fairness he could have done with a little help and to show that I was changing and the change was overwhelming, I thought for a minute second to offer my help and join him behind the bar.

'I knew it was you, I just knew . . . ' The unsmiling chap said on his return.

'Did you now?' I said, rolling up the sleeve of my mind.

He seemed genuinely pleased to see me and was even more thrilled that I had remembered his name of Fitzgibbon and much about him. 'You had a younger brother didn't you?' I asked.

After his first slurp of whiskey, I happily recognised him as being a drunk. For a drunk person is often easier to mould, not unlike warmed-up Plasticine. Ask the offspring of sozzled parents. As long as you catch them at the right moment, before they have crossed that invisible line into vagueness, vitriol or violence, you can ask them for practically anything and receive a positive response.

I recalled Fitzgibbon's younger face, not as attractive as it was now. It had been pudgy with the onset of acne spread over the forehead and a series of black heads covering his nose; amazing how the mind remembers these details. He was never a favourite, never a boy I particularly liked. In fact I remember him as being a bore, and it seemed little had changed. By the time I had remembered he bowled left arm spin and was opening bat, he had returned to the bar three times for refills. The posh girls had sloped off to Luna Caprese, the Italian restaurant across the road.

'I'll join you there,' he had said, reassuring one by gently placing his hands on her head like an ageing bishop at an ordination. After they had giggled out of view he leant over and whispered in his whiskey breath, 'Damn scrubbers.'

I was beginning to worry that he was becoming too drunk too soon, that the character change which I have often witnessed when a person has taken alcohol – heard in a voice, for example, or seen in the eyes, or, yes, witnessed in a mirror, had already taken him beyond the stage at which I could successfully suck out the information I so needed. I had to strike soon, before my young acquaintance became unintelligible. Taking out on the booze, his anger at the cards the universe had dealt, for he moaned on about his job in London and how his boss had not recognised his 'true talent'.

'Not fair,' I added, as a form of fake support. It was all I could muster for this train wreck of a person. All I wanted to ask and to ask again was: 'Have you seen D? Are you friends with him? What does he look like?' For although I looked at his photograph every single morning and acknowledged the beauty of his face, I had made no effort to contact him nor gone out of my way to find

183

out what he had been doing nor how he had grown. I had run into Falston boys before now, some had even attended the tutorial, but never those who had been in D's year, nor had attended the school in the years I had been a teacher; extraordinary but true. I had heard or read that the dear headmaster had been killed in a freak accident on the high street of Ipswich for God's sake! A police car, in answering an emergency call, had lost control and driven straight into the headmaster, who was standing by a lamp post reading a tidbit from the *Evening Star*. Who knows why the bugger was there at that precise moment but I do recall I gave a faint smile on hearing the news.

I felt a shudder pass down my spine, a shiver of evil as the 'bore' moaned on. Enough, enough! Don't spoil my mood, which was inevitably changing for the umpteenth time that day, due to the mix of alcohol: never a good thing even for someone of my experience. I looked at my drink and had a sense, or should I say instinct, that he had injected poison into it with a syringe. Yes, he, too, was part of the plot from those bastards at Falston to scrub my name from its memory. My drink was poisoned, and at that very moment the landlady was arranging for a bed to be made up in the John Radcliffe Hospital, ordering for there to be no bloodstained sheets 'please' and for scalpels to be sharpened and the morgue to be set to appropriate temperature.

It was easy. A sprinkling of arsenic placed round the rim, just like sugar in certain cocktails. Stay calm! Be calm, preferably to think even in poisoned times. Fitzgibbon's laugh became more sinister; I clenched my fist under the table. Pull yourself together Coles. He had returned yet again, this time with an uncorked bottle of red wine. I snatched the wine from off the table, and grabbed the bottle by the neck. I poured him a glass; if I were to be poisoned then he would die as well. I excused myself and I went to the bathroom to heave my guts out.

As I returned to my table, I suddenly remembered Fitz-gibbon's father, who used to sit in a deck chair by the cricket pavilion handing out advice about what others should or should not do or be doing, about how the school should or should not be run, about the direction in which the world should or should not be heading and who generally rued the declining standards, lack of courtesy, cluelessness of modern times and of the up and coming generations, often without variable alternatives. He was the classic prep school parent, a classic horror.

'How is your dear father?' I asked.

Fitzgibbon rather oddly produced a black and white photo of the old bugger, 'He's no longer with us.' I let out a broad smile across my face but thinking he might have seen it, changed my mouth just a fraction to a gasp. I paused and finally said very softly, 'He was a fine man.'

'Do you keep in touch with any of my, rather your, con-temporaries?' I asked, changing the subject and getting to the reason we were talking in the first place.

He leant forward elbow on table, head cupped in one hand, glass in the other. His eyes seemed to roll in syncopation to the steady if slow oscillation of the piped music which before that moment I had never noticed.

'I want to know if I can guess correctly,' he said, with the slight whine of someone just in control. 'What you are really asking is how we all felt when you left the school that afternoon?'

'How did you guess?' I replied, knowing that I would have to wait a little longer before asking directly how or where D was.

He leant further forward, 'We were never told directly, but we all knew, we all knew . . . '

A pregnant silence fell across the table. In fact, there was a quietness as intense as post-coital peace.

'It was more a matter of guessing who your victims were . . . '

'Victims!?'

'Yes, the poor sods you abused Mr Coles.'

There was total silence for a second, in which I may have prayed.

Now that my dear friend was gaining strength, or should we say courage, he carried on with renewed authority. He had become very sober all at once. I could hear the siren of police cars and for a split second my whole cosmic order was suddenly in chaos.

'I know Proudlock was one of your victims . . . '

'Are you going to fucking join us?' – came an unladylike interruption from one of the posh girls who had been stranded in the restaurant over the road. Dear, dear I thought, 'The higher the social class, the worse the manners.'

'Not right now!' He spat in her direction, with such authority that she recoiled back out of the door like some pet bitch.

'Too much drink, that's all,' he said, as a form of explanation to his sudden outburst.

'As I was saying, Proudlock was a victim and then the guessing game began on who else . . . '

'What made you think that all the gossip was true? How do you know that it was not made up? Schoolboy tittle-tattle? A conspiracy leaked by a jealous master?'

'Let's just say that I know.'

We sat in another uncomfortable silence, one in which angels did not pass overhead, so much as gremlins underneath. I shuffled embarrassedly. I reckoned that I might have already revealed too much for my own good. Not with my words but through my eyes.

His mouth was wide open. I was in the hope that some pearls of wisdom would exude; but instead he said something that I still find hard to believe.

'He told me that you raped him. He only told me last year. You see he feels shame of what was done; he feels complicit. He

186

was eleven years-old and he still feels complicit in your rape.' His mood had gone from happy drunk to dark menacing hate. I felt a shoelace of sweat on my brow.

'I beg your pardon,' I said a touch annoyed. 'I beg your pardon,' was all I could think of. I went in search for an honest fist of a fact, an excuse, reason, explanation, justification, take your pick!

His venom took me by surprise. I fumbled for words like looking for a light switch in the dark.

'What were you thinking? Did you for a moment think what you were doing? How profoundly you would mar his life, even in some respects destroy it?'

'Rubbish!' I snapped. Images throbbed in my drunken head with the regularity of a woodpecker. 'If something hurts enough, we do something about it, eh?'

He finally screamed, 'He was eleven years-old!'

'I think you will find Proudlock was thirteen years-old.'

'I was not talking about Proudlock.'

And then I realised he was talking about D.

'Who the fuck do you think you are?' I replied. I acknowledge the reality that doubt, fear, hate, probably all negative feeling, is sometimes the result not so much of one's being human, as of one's being sick, incapable of facing oneself and life as they are, and therefore obliged to drink more and more and more and more, and therefore becoming sicker and sicker, and sicker and sicker, as if trapped on another bolting carousel that will one day CRASH. 'Before wagging the finger, young man, I would look in the mirror; what you will see is not very impressive.'

I promise I wanted to be honest about how I felt. But still I hesitated. One part of me did want to reveal myself – warts and all. What have I to lose, the clock has struck? Another part of me says that a gratuitous excess of honesty can be the shining of another torch into the other's eye or like shouting directly into a person's hearing aid. Surely it is better for those you have met or will meet, that there is a measure of aloofness, even anonymity, so that others are allowed to assess the details for themselves. Should I or should I not?

It was as if the Falston boy had read my mind as his tone softened and he looked straight into my eyes and said, 'It is never too late to tell the truth, is it?'

And I admit, hearing these words I was scared shitless. So what did I do but to 'open up' to this stranger, a boy I once taught; I felt forty years younger just doing so. I remember being chased up the stairs by my father. He was a thin man, an accountant by trade and in his suit and tie, looked sterile. He thumped on my bedroom door, "OPEN UP! I KNOW YOU ARE IN THERE!" My mother and sister had gone out and we were alone in the house. I had pinned a wicker chair under the handle and it had locked or at least offered resistance. I had seen it done during the Sunday movie only two days before which we watched as a happy suburban family. Knock, knock, thump. I lay rigid in the corner, trying not to breathe, throat tickling, heart pounding. Knock, knock, thump, and suddenly my door, my protection, seemed as flimsy as the gardener's shed at the bottom of the garden. It would soon break open from the sheer repetitiveness of the knocking, like a piece of metal that is bent forwards and backwards, forwards and backwards until . . . it snaps!

'Who is it?' I asked quietly, letting go of my breath. 'Who is it?'

'It's me!' my father replied. 'Let me in!'

I opened the door with care, one foot against the base, ready to slam it shut, just in case. My father barged in and immediately shut the door behind. And he replaced the wicker chair as a lock in one speedy action that immediately told me what was about to happen; I had no chance for escape. My father was breathing heavily. Inhale. Exhale. Inhale. Exhale Slowly. Regularly. Reaching that stage of not breathing but being breathed, like that book which you do not read but reads you. He shoved me against my bed; there was no care, no warmth. 'STOP!' I yelled and pleaded, and he hurt me and at first I thought of nothing, of nothing, not a thing and then I thought that he was killing me and my heart sunk. I swear I thought he was the foul beast with forty tails. I felt as lonely as one does when waiting for a coffin to be carried out of a house to a hearse or from a hearse into a church. I remember him chuckling softly as he went out of the room . . . For days I was lost for words, as if winded by a blow to the stomach. 'What is wrong with you?' my mother would ask and I had no answer and kept quiet. I had no intention of revealing what had happened and what was going to happen for the next seven years of my life, until I was thirteen years-old.

'So don't you come up and accuse me of doing this and doing that,' I said. 'Anyone is capable of doing the most appalling things, I learnt that very early. It is how you deal with it. I can tell you now that your friend was only treated with the upmost respect and care. I looked after him, nothing more, and nothing less. He was the lucky one; in the end, he let ME down.'

The Falston boy hesitated and raised his eyes, which were a mix of repulsion and sorrow. He straightened his jacket and literally bit his knuckle. I must have hit a raw nerve, several raw nerves. He exposed what I secretly think some people secretly think of me, those people being the ones I most secretly blame for turning me into what I think they secretly think of me.

We then sat in silence till he blurted out an answer to what he assumed was the question I had wanted to ask.

'You cannot go on using forever the age-old excuse that we are what we are because of fate; that everything is predestined by genes and fashioned by early upbringing; that we have no real chance of becoming different.'

189

"Nothing much of importance happens after the age of six," laments the sour old bitch. "Get them before seven, and they've some chance of heaven," smirks the priest. "Before the age of eight, or else it's too late," frothed the paedophile. I challenge such hypotheses by saying that there comes a time when we, all of us, must stand up and be counted, when we can no longer resort to that readily available but readily avoidable grand reason of: "It was how we were made, how we were born, how we were taught." A moment arrives when we need to make a decision to decide for ourselves what to decide for ourselves; when we each become responsible for what we do, and for the consequences of it; and for how we think. Although we may not be responsible for what we are taught, we are responsible for what we now believe is wrong yet which we condone, actively encourage, or ignore. To quote: "The truth is replaced by silence, and the silence is a lie". We may not be responsible for previous foul or ignorant actions, but we are responsible if we repeat them. We may not be responsible for the thoughts that come into our heads, but we are responsible for those we let stay there.'

He banged the table with his fist, the last post sounded: 'You remind me of a worm, Mr Coles, which even when cut into pieces wriggles away in different sections and directions. I feel no sorrow, only hate and pity. Falston is celebrating its 100th year next Friday and our, rather my friend, will be there. I admit to you here and now that I am unsure whether I will reveal that we have even met.' With that he picked up his glass and finished his drink. 'Do you know the saddest part of his story was when he described having to face his father? The headmaster had summoned five sets of parents he thought should be informed that you had been sacked. The parents of the boys he believed you were closest to. You see it was not our friend who had given your game away – it was Proudlock.'

I was shocked not only by the suddenness of the revelation

but how it had been revealed in so matter of fact a way. I was too ashamed to weep, worse to be caught weeping at that moment. Sweep under the carpet, Coles, press it down, hold it in, laugh it off.

'When the parents arrived, the headmaster told them what had happened and his concern for other children.' I tried to interrupt. He shook his hand as if to say: 'Shut up, Coles, do not move a muscle, nothing would give me greater pleasure than to smack my fist in the middle of your face!' He hoisted himself from the table, 'Afterwards his father asked him if you had done anything inappropriate. His father looked directly into his eyes and said, "My darling boy, you would tell me if he ever laid a hand on you." D replied without a moment's hesitation, "No, father, he did nothing." '

'You see Mr Coles, you groomed him so well that you had broken him, not only from his family, but from the truth.'

*   *   *

Holy quote: 'Fear knocked at the door. Faith opened. And there was nothing there.'

The car was parked not far from the Falston gate. Friday the thirteenth, considered being unlucky especially for those suffering from triskaidekaphobia, but it need not, not for me.

I had driven from Oxford, my first drive for five years. The landlady had offered her Golf and I had muttered a 'thank you.' As I set off to Norfolk, I had turned up its radio. The tune in my head drowned the music from the speakers. I had not been the same since my meeting in the Rose and Crown. I had underrated his bluster, his drink! A malaise had fallen over me since that day. It had taken me by surprise and since then I had woken with a louder, more terrifying groan than ever before. I had tried a number of times to cheer myself up by not dwelling on the memory of less glorious moments such as using

191

my cupboard as a toilet, urinating on my mattress, vomiting on my shirt – all drink-related I state in my defence – but above all the dances I have had with some friends and students. I admit, and it is and was the first time, I had felt shame. That drunkard over-bearing Falston slob had lanced images that had remained buried in my mind. What do they say? 'If you have a skeleton in your wardrobe, take it out and dance with it.'

My Falston friend had let it slip that the school would be celebrating their hundredth year. The birthday celebration felt more like a funeral; I had even dressed in my dark ministerial suit and black tie. The suit I had worn when I first met D around the same time of year. How handsome and confident I must have seemed that day, but I now sat alone in a clapped-out car without even a fucking invitation.

I had no plan other than to watch the old boys drift into the school and then join the celebrations when they had started. I had rung the school and a shrill voice had answered and coldly informed that there was to be a service of celebration in the chapel at 7.00 pm followed by dinner in the hall.

'You must bring your invitation, please don't forget it,' the patronising cow insisted.

'Do you expect gatecrashers?' I asked mockingly.

'Well, you never know do you?'

A group of cars started to turn into the gates, one by one returning to their school days; a conspiratorial group if ever I had witnessed. I watched like a member of a neighbourhood watch as my stomach ached, salving the secrets of my conscience. Somehow being in the presence of my past made things easier to deal with.

'Come on hurry up,' I kept repeating to myself. 'I can't just sit out here and wait.' I decided to drive in, enough of this damn fear. There was no invitation but that was irrelevant. I was invited due to my past service, end of debate. I put my foot down, swung the car to the right, and joined a small queue through the school gates; home at last!

I was beckoned forward to 'park over there'. The man issuing the orders was the science teacher. He looked at me with surprise, verging on shock.

'Thank you,' I said, as nonchalantly as possible. I thought for a moment that he was going to report my arrival but I remember him being a weak human being so I marched up to him and said, 'Wipe that surprise from your face and keep your nose out of things that do not concern you.'

'Of course, Mr Coles,' he whimpered, as his expression darkened as if clouding over with amazement and anger. Poor fool!

The familiar buildings made my balance uneasy as if I were carrying a tray in one hand whilst closing the door with the other. I had presumed that I would recognise many but by the time I reached the hall I felt like an outsider invited to the wrong party. I had to galvanise my courage, 'Be strong Coles,' I kept repeating to myself. I remembered at that moment some useful advice my father had once passed on to me: 'If people frighten you, imagine them in the bath with their rubber duck.'

As the hall was filling, I took the opportunity to go on a tour of the school. How it had changed, in the way things do when we return to a previous chapter of our life. Everything seemed smaller, more compact and bland. The staff room was empty and as expected for such an occasion, spotless; everything straightened, books piled neatly on top of each other. I walked over to my old desk, which was bare as if waiting for my return and was amazed to find a yellow frame that I had bought years before still hanging on a wall, to its side. It read 'WHEN NO ONE IS IN AUTHORITY, THE PEOPLE BREAK LOOSE.'

'Hello, Coles, what the hell are you doing here?'

It was Jeremy Thomas, the French teacher, not looking so

youthful. I did not answer, instead continued my inspection of my old office.

'I bought this from Mundesley,' I said holding up the frame.

The banter continued into a non-discussion about nothing in particular, swerving all over the place, from this to that and back again, like dodgems at a funfair. Most important from my point of view was that the conversation was not dominated with my past and yet, as he was about to leave to join the party, he seemed to count to ten as it were, in his case a very short ten.

He whispered in a very loud whisper, 'You really shouldn't be here old boy. I think you better go. It is a big occasion and you may well soil it by your presence.' He continued, 'What you did was inexcusable. I mean really old boy, you let the whole side down.'

I saw clearly that he was trying to be civil but the tightening of his knuckles gave the game away.

'I better be going, the whole shebang starts in twenty odd minutes,' he said, nervously glancing at his wrist with no watch strapped to it. He shook his head, 'Never wear one these days, it reminds me too much of death!'

Then quite suddenly, he repeated what he had said before, 'You let the whole bloody side down. Now please go.' At first it was old boy this and old boy that, all softly spoken, good to see you and then wallop! He was telling me to exit with a bang. 'After you left we, the masters, were interrogated as if we were all paedophiles. You knew the unwritten rule, look but never touch.'

'But it's no good looking at the goods if you can't touch them,' I replied instinctively and then uttered fleetingly under my breath: '*godwhycreateoursexdriveandthenmakeusfeelbadaboutit?*'

He looked at me in astonishment. Come Mr Thomas, don't act the innocent with me. I then recited a friend's quote: 'The only near perfect people are saints, and most of them are dead.' But another voice urged: Cannot sex also be beautiful, educative, capable of expanding the normal person's tedious two, or perhaps three position repertoire! And is not the expression on a beautifully fucked face, after all, that of a triumph? It is a victory of trust. It brings honourable tears and a detachment from God, depending on your definition of God. Assuming you are fortunate or whatever enough to have found, or to have had found, such a known and loved person in your life.

'But standards must be maintained as our new headmaster is keen to convey,' was Thomas' parting shot. Before I could throw one more quote: 'Being on the tightrope is living; everything else is waiting', he had scurried away without even a goodbye.

Damn him and damn this new morality. It may have been twenty years since I last walked in this building but I get the distinct impression the school had steadily fallen behind. I should be the headmaster welcoming everyone today; instead I cower away from the crowd like an illness lurking deep within some body.

As I walked the corridors, I glanced at the school photographs, lined against the dirty green walls. I went in search for my year and on seeing my youthful face sitting just two places away from the headmaster and in front of the house cup, I was overcome and took one from the wall and broke its glass and ripped the photograph in two, as in truth, I could not accept what had happened to me since then and since them.

I was beginning to lose heart; maybe this was not such a good idea. I must keep moving, stop pausing at every classroom, every desk. The modern world needs fast literature, fast action, fast characters, fast life, fast results. Modern people want short-term solutions, the quick fix, microwave ovens, charismatic religion, hotlines to God, entertainment at a click. Perhaps I had lost pace with this new world. They need immediate sex, to hell with the wooing and courting; I have read that even foreplay is outdated. But then a voice soothed 'Keep going!' and 'This is where you belong,' and even, 'Come on, forgive and forget,' followed by a quick, 'you must be fucking joking.'

I headed towards the dormitories and found D's bed. The bed was made; a tartan blanket, similar to the one he held, had been hurriedly flung on. Its shape resembled a corpse that was of the same length and shape as D, it was as if he were there waiting for me. I took him into my arms, and squeezed him gently, the pained but passionate partner of a warrior who had been away too long.

I carried him to my room, my mind, body, and soul cushioning each step. I lay him down on my bed and heard myself cry. I gave him the briefest kiss as if we were in a nursery story tale. The flight of the sun passed momentarily by the window and broke through lighting the white of the walls causing D's ghostly figure to become whiter than snow.

*   *   *

A cheesy song greeted my discreet entrance into the back of the hall. As I looked around for familiar faces, it seemed that my boys had grown nearly beyond recognition. They induced a nostalgia I feel when I see fading flowers that soon will be pulled from a vase. They reminded me of a line of ducklings, most ugly except the one at the back. His head raised, body rigid, his chin pointing halfway to the sky. I could see a pulse throb in his temple; it is D. Careful what you pray for, you might get it! The agony of fruition exceeds the cold sweat of expectation. And I then sighed with relief to discover a blemish on what I thought for one ghastly and ghostly moment was perfection itself, even if it – the blemish – be the tiny error deliberately woven into an exquisite carpet.

The hall fell silent as the new headmaster stood to perform his 'the finest school in the world' speech; my mind was still elsewhere. I certainly heard his monotonous voice drone on and even I looked into his henpecked face as he boringly spouted each line, each word sitting on the predictable fence. If only this had been me I would have stolen quote after quote, but aren't all quotes by their very definition stolen? It was Churchillian in delivery to help the gathered truly understand how privileged their lives had been: 'If it had been great all the time we wouldn't know how great it is.' I looked again into the headmaster's eyes and BANG, without warning, started to buckle, grabbing an armrest in front to maintain my balance. Dear Mother of God, it could not have been, surely not? But it was, without question. It was the geography master who had risen from the lowly ranks of perversity to become headmaster of Falston. Shame, shame, on him and shame on the fucking world!

A murder of 'why's' spewed out of my mouth, but this time were answered by a short sharp shot: WHY NOT!

And my mind tried to appease once more with a friendly old quote: 'Oh why, oh why, oh why, oh why, why, oh why, oh why?'

'Because, because, because, because.'

'Goodbye, goodbye, goodbye.'

*   *   *

That is the last I remember until I woke abruptly with an ache in my stomach at the remembrance of something so horrible that I wanted to go immediately back to sleep. But I sat up with the awareness that I was being watched. My head spun as

I began to focus my eyes. The geography master, or should I say, headmaster, was handing me a glass of water.

'You collapsed,' he said shaking his head. 'We don't have long, the parents are waiting.'

'Pour me a drink will you?' I asked through bleary eyes, my mouth as dry as the bottom of a parrot's cage.

He handed me a glass of water.

'And what's this?'

'It is a glass of water,' he answered. 'Now listen Coles, what the hell are you doing here? I hope you haven't come to cause trouble.'

'I came to visit my old school, celebrate its centenary and to see D.'

'He was never going to be here, you fool.'

'But I saw him.'

'You were imagining it. He won't be coming back to this school.'

'I saw him!' I paused, asking myself whether he was telling the truth. Why should he lie? I began to feel like my whole life was a lie, that I could no longer believe my own eyes. My shoulders felt heavy.

The geography teacher took a step forward; shut his eyes for an instant then spoke, 'He has too many ghosts. He won't want them disturbed, certainly not until his parents die. You see we are safe until then, I know that. Children don't want to hurt their mummy and daddy, to make them feel guilty that somehow they had let their children down by sending them away at so early an age. By the time they want to moan, too many years have gone by and many simply don't believe it. "Figment of the boy's imagination, attention seeker!" Don't forget every parent thinks it can never happen at their children's school. That is why today is a celebration, Coles, a hundred years of good old-fashioned school mastering.'

I thought I heard the headmaster grunt like he'd received a sudden punch in the chest and then slowly he licked his lips. 'We are charming, considerate and appear like everybody else. We are in the perfect place. Well I am. You foolishly blew it by, should we say, over doing things.'

I had underrated the geography master, 'You are a monster!' I sneered.

'And you are not, Mr Coles? Don't forget, you not only taught the boys, the fact of the matter is you also taught me.'

'The first fact of the matter, headmaster, is that people who know fuck-all what they are talking about tend to use expressions like "the fact of the matter is". The second fact of the matter is, headmaster, alias pervert or whatever you are now calling yourself, is that it doesn't matter what you really think because I know you are living a lie, petrified that someone will expose you for the charlatan you really are!'

I suddenly felt a tightening of the chest and started to take shallow breaths, trying to breathe evenly and steadily . . . evenly and steadily, shoulders back. I took a gulp of water.

'Don't die on me Coles, not here anyway.'

And whilst he spoke, I heard the thudding footsteps and hot breath of the parents on the nape of my neck. It might well have been a further figment of my imagination, but I also understood that the real steps were very near.

'As I said, I have to be going. The new boys are waiting to hear me say grace for dinner; I will quietly pray for you Mr Coles.'

'And, headmaster, I will pray for the wisdom to differentiate between those whom you should respect and emulate, even venerate, and those whom you should suspect and reject, even despise.'

*   *   *

By the time I reached the hotel, the day had faded and the night had set. I had booked into the no star Sea View Hotel, a dreary three-storey terraced house overlooking the flat black North Sea. A small red neon sign shone brightly 'Vacancies' from the ground floor window and for an instant, as I drove up, I thought I had arrived at one of the local brothels.

The debris from one of the last days of summer was being cleared. I felt as if I were in the wrong place at the wrong time. My room at the top of the house was sparse and battle ship grey.

'The best in the hotel,' the proprietor cheerfully announced as he opened the door. I had not brought any luggage except a wash bag just in case I had been invited to dinner and needed a second shave. On reflection that was pure nonsense, I had brought it along to carry my load of prescription pills. I had managed to order three month's worth instead of the prescribed four week's supply. I had explained to the pharmacist that I was travelling and he had not bothered to ask for any proof. I slumped on to the bed and wondered what it is that decides who must die, and when, and how and why. I had opened my window and felt a gentle breeze whispering an answer that I was unable to hear.

'WHAT IS THE ANSWER?' I yelled and inhaled a lungful of my last sea air. A bird suddenly rested on the windowsill. It looked grim and grey, not unlike the coast line itself. It looked like death was coming to greet me.

I counted out the pills in the way that I used to count my Smarties when I was small. Yes, when I was young, innocent, and untouched. One, two, three, four . . .

I will sleep now.

I will sleep a sleep that no sound of the world will disturb, nor all the faces of all the boys I have taught, nor those whom I have guided, nor those whom I have wronged, nor the thought of D, of D . . . of D.